To Sophie May
Hope you enjoy Mia's story
Thanks for your support.
With love Shelley Wilson x

SHELLEY WILSON

OATH BREAKER

a novel

LIVONIA, MICHIGAN

OATH BREAKER

Published by H2O
an imprint of BHC Press

Library of Congress Control Number:
2017933756

ISBN-13: 978-1-946006-67-7
ISBN-10: 1-946006-67-X

www.bhcpress.com

ALSO BY
SHELLEY WILSON

FICTION TITLES

Guardians of the Dead
Book 1 of The Guardians

Guardians of the Sky
Book 2 of The Guardians

Guardians of the Lost Lands
Book 3 of The Guardians

NON-FICTION TITLES

How I Changed My Life in a Year
Meditation for Beginners
Vision Boards for Beginners
Motivate Me! Oracle Guidebook

ANTHOLOGIES

In Creeps The Night: An Anthology
Featuring "The House On The Hill"
by S.L. Wilson

For Ella

The scariest monsters
are the ones that lurk
within our souls.

~ Edgar Allan Poe ~

ONE

The blue flashing lights pulsed through the fractured front window, illuminating the blood splatter on the walls. The click-click of the forensic team's camera ate into the sterile silence as the officers combed through the living room.

Like something out of a macabre horror show the blood covered everything, coating the threadbare rug in front of the fireplace with its crimson wash. The splintered remains of the coffee table littered the overturned chair, and the smell of death clung to the walls.

I lifted my eyes to look at the police officer who knelt in front of me, his face a mask of professionalism even though he must be wishing he was anywhere but here.

'Did you see who killed your dad?' I slowly shook my head as the officer tried to determine what had happened.

'Someone tried to kill you, miss. I want to help. Did you see who broke in and attacked you?'

I couldn't answer. The words were stuck in my throat. How could I tell him that my dad was the one who tried to kill me and that a wolf had jumped through the window and ripped out his throat? Who would believe me?

The paramedic dropped a medical kit at my feet and began wiping the blood from my face, the sudden cold of the antiseptic wipe causing an involuntary shudder to run through my bones. The police officer and paramedic exchanged a look. The same kind of look that my teacher and headmaster used to give each other when I tried to cover up the bruises down my arms.

I slumped a little further into the kitchen chair, letting my long dark hair fall around my face.

'Anything you can give us by way of a description will help.' The police officer clicked the end of his pen and poised it over the clean sheet of notepaper.

'Big,' I managed to say. My lips cracked as I spoke, and I could feel a trickle of blood slide down the side of my mouth. The paramedic wiped it up before moving to the gash on my forehead.

'It...he was big. Dark hair. Brown eyes.'

The officer noted it down and let out a deep sigh. Not the best description for them to go on, but it was all I could give him. If I'd told him the attacker was hairy, with sharp claws and fangs, the paramedic would have had me committed. I didn't need to escape from one prison to then find myself in another.

'It's late. Who can we call?' the medic asked as he secured a small bandage to my head. 'Any family?'

The police officer grabbed the radio from his shirt pocket. 'I've already called social services. As she's a minor we need to find her a bed for the night. I'll chase them up.'

'No!' I could hear the flicker of panic in my voice as the threat of being sent away loomed. 'I can call my brother. He'll let me stay with him. He's much older than me and has his own place. It'll be fine.'

They exchanged another look.

'What's his number and we'll call him for you?'

Shit.

I hadn't seen Zak since he walked out nine years ago. He'd promised to come back for me but he never did. He left me alone with that bastard who called himself our father.

'I'll find it,' I mumbled, standing up and moving towards the living room. The police officer barred the door.

'It's probably best that you don't enter the crime scene, miss. You've been through enough tonight already, so why don't you take a seat and tell me where to look?'

Double shit.

I needed to stall for time. If only someone were willing to lie to the police about being my brother then I wouldn't have to go with the social worker. Unfortunately, friends were a luxury I never got to enjoy.

My heart beat faster as I wrestled with the possibility of leaving this house. If I went with them, Zak would never be able to find me. I stumbled against the dresser, knocking a vase to the floor with a loud crash.

The paramedic led me back to the plastic kitchen chair and I lowered myself into it, resting my head on the wooden table and letting my long hair fan out around me. The softly murmured voices of the police officer and the medic washed over me as I closed my eyes.

Throat torn open—blood gushing from the wound as it sprayed across the furniture—his eyes wide in shock and panic as he fell to the floor.

Keeping my head on the table, I tuned into the conversations around me. The officers were speculating on the attacker, trying to understand how someone could cause that much carnage.

Strong assailant—nothing missing—bloody mess—no chance of survival.

They went on, talking through all the possibilities. Of course, none of them came close to the truth—how could they?

I squeezed my eyes more tightly shut as I tried to block out the images that danced across the inside of my eyelids. His eyes. The blood.

A man's deep voice cut through the air and a shudder skittered down my spine. The sharp tone and arrogance reminded me of my father, and I had to lift my head to check he hadn't risen from the dead.

I opened my eyes and blinked against the stark brightness of the kitchen light.

'This is Sebastian Roberts, miss.' The police officer led him into the room.

The well-dressed man filled the kitchen doorway; his dark suit and long overcoat looked as if they cost more than my dad earned in a year. His shoes shone in the bright light of the kitchen, and I instinctively tucked my tatty trainers under the chair.

I figured him to be middle-aged and he had thick black hair that was neatly clipped around a square face. The hard lines of his nose and jaw worked to highlight the cold grey eyes that stared down at me.

'He says he's your uncle.' The police officer gestured for Mr Roberts to take a seat, but he remained where he was, watching me with predatory eyes.

I'd only met this man a couple of times when I was a kid, but the striking resemblance to my father would have convinced anyone that he was who he said he was. They could have been twins apart from the difference in hair colour and the small fact that this man was clean-shaven and professional, and my father had been a drunken mess with a violent temper.

'We were about to call her brother to come and get her.'

My uncle huffed. '*If* Mia's brother gets in touch, then do feel free to pass on my details so he can come and visit her at my home.' Sebastian Roberts looked pointedly at me as he said it, and I understood immediately that I was busted. He knew I didn't have a clue where Zak was.

Shit.

•• • ● • ••

THE POLICE OFFICER took Sebastian to one side as his female colleague escorted me towards the stairs to pack a bag and collect anything I needed. I took my time ascending the steps as I strained to overhear their conversation.

'Is there a number where you can be reached, sir?'

'Of course. Here's a business card with my direct number and the address where Mia will be staying for the time being.'

Where I would be staying remained a mystery to me. The only flicker of hope I could hold onto was that it couldn't be any worse than here.

As I gazed around my dismal bedroom, it struck me what a pathetic life I had led so far. A handful of books, some of my mum's handwritten poetry that I'd managed to salvage after she died, underwear, four tops and two pairs of jeans. My worldly belongings fit into one backpack. I avoided looking directly at the female officer as she glanced around the dank bedroom. The pity on her face was almost too much to bear. Staying in this house was supposed to have been temporary. Zak had promised that he would come back for me. I didn't need a new bed or lots of pretty things, not if I needed to get away quickly when he came. Of course, he never had come back to get me.

I gave a sharp nod to indicate that I was done, and we made our way back down to the kitchen.

Sebastian was waiting by a large black car when I arrived. The medic pressed a spare bandage into my hand as I stepped out of the front door, and the police officer gave a grim nod of his head as I walked towards him.

15

'We'll be in touch, miss,' he told me. I didn't care if he did get in touch. I just wished this whole brutal night would disappear from my memory, but I forced a smile and whispered my thanks.

The fresh night air settled around me like a cloak, the sky dotted with grey clouds that swept across the full moon, its creamy light bathing the front garden in an eerie glow.

Sebastian watched me as I trudged down the path and joined him on the passenger side.

'We have a long drive ahead of us, Mia.' He opened the door. 'We better get started.'

I didn't look back. I didn't want to see the broken window or the blood splattered across the walls. The neighbours had congregated on the pavement and were watching the events unfold. I avoided their staring faces as I slid into the leather seat and closed the door.

The tinted windows offered me some comfort as the black car slid past the gawping faces. I shut my eyes and let the exhaustion creep over me.

•• • ● • ••

THE SOUND OF the car engine cutting out stirred me from a frenzied dream of blood, teeth and carnage, and I was grateful for the reprieve as the whirlwind of images steamrolled through my brain. Sebastian sat motionless at the wheel and stared ahead through the windscreen.

'Are we here?' I wasn't quite sure where *here* was, as my mysterious uncle had been a bit vague on our destination. I'd been too distracted to bother asking and now my uneasiness troubled me.

He grunted and shifted his gaze to look over at me, his eyes sweeping over my face and hovering on the split lip and bandaged forehead.

'Not yet. We've been driving most of the night, and I thought you might need a bathroom break.'

He had stopped at the motorway services. I noticed the glass-fronted building in the distance and saw the steady stream of people rushing in and out. The car park was busy with motorists in need of a caffeine fix before resuming their journey. The flickering sign for beverages beckoned to me, and I sat up straight in my seat.

'I could do with a coffee.'

We entered the building side by side but in silence. I didn't know this man and he didn't know me. If I was going to spend the next God knew how long with him, I needed to open my mouth and at least attempt to hold a conversation with him.

'Two white coffees.' He handed over the cash, ignoring the pleasant smile from the barista as he motioned for us to sit in a free booth.

'I'm not sure that sixteen-year-olds should drink coffee.'

I almost laughed.

'You don't have kids?'

'No, my brother was the sibling graced with offspring.'

I did laugh at that.

'I don't think my dad thought he had been *graced* with anything.' I stirred my coffee a little too violently and watched as it slopped over the rim and left a muddy puddle on the table.

'Your father had a lot to deal with. The death of his wife, the loss of his son. It all took its toll on his mental health and...'

'How dare you.' I dropped the teaspoon with a clatter as I raised my voice. A couple of patrons glanced in our direction.

'What do *you* know about our life? Dad was a bastard, plain and simple. These bruises were from him and they weren't the first. They wouldn't have been the last either if that...if he hadn't been killed.'

I dropped my gaze and lifted the coffee cup to my lips. My hands shook slightly as I let my little outburst settle. I'd never done that in the past. I'd never verbalised what my dad had done, even when my teachers tried so hard to get me to admit it. It all went back to Zak. If I had spoken out about the violence, social services would have taken me away. Zak wouldn't have been able to find me when the time came. I couldn't risk that happening, so I kept my mouth shut.

'I'm sorry.'

Sebastian's words surprised me.

'What have you got to be sorry about? He was the bad one, not you.' I realised that there was every possibility that Sebastian was also a bad one. Could this be a family gene?

As if reading my mind, he began to shake his head.

'I'm nothing like my brother, Mia. You are perfectly safe with me. The death of your mother changed him in ways none of us could understand. He was such a kind man once. A long time ago.'

'Well, I must have been out that day because I never saw any kindness, not a single moment of it.'

I wanted to say more, but as I opened my mouth to speak his phone began vibrating in his pocket.

'I need to take this. I'll be back soon.'

With that he stood up and walked away, his mobile pressed up to his ear.

•• • ● • ••

THE SMELL OF diesel and strong coffee assaulted my senses. I took another sip of the hot liquid and screwed my eyes shut. I'd never really liked coffee, but I opted for it in a bid to convince Sebastian that I was a sophisticated teenager. Why I believed that drinking a cup of coffee would make me look less of a child was a mystery to me. I remember seeing it on a TV show once. Road to nowhere and a cup of coffee, please. Stupid. As he was paying, I should have gone for the hot chocolate with extra cream.

The tiny screen above the entrance showed the network of motorways, giving out up-to-date advice on scheduled roadworks and estimated travel times. The southbound route was busy, even at this time of night, with a flow of vehicles heading to the capital. The traffic heading north was much lighter. North; I had a faint memory of Zak telling me that he wanted to go to Scotland. He had shown me a map once, trailing his index finger up to the centre of the United Kingdom and tapping the spot over the county of Nottinghamshire.

'This is the belly button of the UK,' he had said. 'I'm going to start here and work my way up north until I make it to the Scottish mountains.'

Zak's need for adventure was palpable. Being outdoorsy kids, we thrived on that glimpse of freedom. I only wish that I'd been allowed to venture further than the garden gate more often.

We both loved the smell of the trees after a rainstorm, and lying on the grass to watch the clouds or the stars in the sky.

We had been brought up in a colossal concrete jungle. Grey boxes stacked on top of each other with a token patch of green grass at the centre of each estate. The trees were dead and the animals were either feral cats or angry dogs.

I shifted in my seat as I tried to shake the memory of home, or rather, the house I had lived in. My thoughts were interrupted when a young man placed a steaming mug of hot chocolate in front of me.

'Can I join you?' He didn't wait for an answer but slid into the space opposite and took a long drink from his own mug.

'Please.' He gestured for me to drink. 'It looks like you need an injection of chocolate.'

The skin around his mouth crinkled when he smiled and his front teeth were slightly crooked. I guessed him to be in his early twenties.

'It's a gift,' he continued as he nodded at the cup. 'A simple act of kindness.'

I fidgeted in my seat and looked around for Sebastian.

'People aren't kind and gifts don't exist,' I said, pushing the mug away and waiting for the explosion of anger that normally accompanied my backchat.

'Hmm, I see.' He put his own mug down and laced his fingers together, studying me with mysterious brown eyes that seemed much older than the face they occupied. His gaze rested only briefly on my split lip.

'You don't believe in acts of kindness?'

I shook my head, my hair swishing around my shoulders.

'No, I don't. Nobody does anything without wanting something in return.'

'So if I offer you a hot chocolate what do you suppose I want in return?'

I sat back in my chair and squared my shoulders. The gravity of a sixteen-year-old girl sitting in a service station all alone in the middle of the night suddenly hit me.

'My uncle will be here any minute and he won't be pleased to find you in his seat.'

'I've scared you,' he said, holding his hands up. 'I'm sorry, that wasn't my intention. I was looking for a bit of light conversation to pass the time, that's all.'

He picked up his mug and took another gulp, his eyes still fixed on me.

'I'm sorry,' I whispered. 'I didn't mean to be rude. I'm...' I stopped myself from opening up to this mysterious stranger.

Reaching for the mug, I smiled weakly at the young man. 'Thank you for the hot chocolate.'

He watched me as I sipped my drink.

'I'm Terry.' He extended his hand across the table and I took it, shaking it firmly just as Zak had taught me.

'I'm Mia.'

'So Mia, where are you heading on this chilly morning?'

I hesitated; regardless of the sweet, hot chocolatey gesture I needed to lie to this guy. I wasn't ready to spill all the gruesome details of my screwed-up life, especially to a stranger.

'I'm going to Scotland.'

He raised his eyebrows and let out a long, low whistle. 'That's a hell of a long journey.'

I laughed at his expression and managed to relax my posture, realising for the first time how tense I was.

'I'm visiting my brother, and he lives in the Scottish mountains.'

Terry cocked his head to one side as if weighing up my answer.

'How do you know he lives in the mountains?'

I blinked. 'Excuse me?'

'How do you know your brother lives in the Scottish mountains? Did he tell you?'

I shook myself out of the shocked silence and stammered a reply, 'Yes...he told me.'

The fact that Zak had only mentioned Scotland to me nine years ago didn't matter. It was the first thing that had popped into my head. This conversation was making me feel uncomfortable, and I looked around again for any sign of Sebastian.

Terry slipped out of his chair, and I curled my fists ready to fend off an attack, but he smiled and moved towards the exit.

As he reached the door, he glanced back at me.

'You might be interested to know that your brother is closer than you think, Mia. I wouldn't bother going all the way to Scotland. Perhaps stay close to the belly button, and be careful who you trust.' He winked and then he was gone.

The gasp froze on my lips. The 'belly button' was Zak's phrase.

I flew out of my seat and rushed to the door, stumbling over my own feet as I went. The cold air hit my face as soon as I stepped outside. I scanned the car park for Terry, but he was nowhere to be seen.

'Mia?'

I whirled around to find Sebastian standing behind me, his posture rigid, deep grooves trailing along his forehead.

'I…I was worried about you,' I lied. 'Thought you'd dumped me and run.'

My eyes continued to roam the car park.

'I'm sorry. It was a business call that couldn't wait.'

I trailed after him as we made our way back to the car. Sliding into the seat, I scoured the dark corners, the parked cars and the surrounding area for any sign of Terry.

Hope filled my chest like a helium balloon.

There was only one way that he could know about Zak's quirky phrase. Whoever this guy was, he knew my brother, and if that was the case, then my brother knew where I was.

SHELLEY WILSON

TWO

When Sebastian told the police that I would be staying with him, I'd pictured a semi-detached house with a front lawn and overgrown flower borders. As he pulled through the tall, wrought-iron gates and into the winding driveway of a stately home, I began to feel slightly cheated. How could he live in such a grand place while my dad barely scraped enough together to afford the dirty hovel that I'd called home?

'It's a school,' he mumbled, as if sensing my animosity.

Panic gripped me and my fingers tightened around the car seat. I was briefly reminded of Terry's warning about who I should trust.

'You're dumping me into a boarding school?'

'No, Mia, this is my home. I run this school for gifted girls.'

I snorted. 'I'm sorry to disappoint you but I'm not gifted. In fact, my grades are about as good as my conversational skills.'

Sebastian huffed, the stony exterior wavering momentarily but snapping back into place as he stopped the car in front of two huge wooden doors.

'I apologise. I should have forewarned you about the nature of my job and home, but Hood Academy is not for the academically gifted, Mia, it's for the physically gifted.'

'What, like a prep school for Miss United Kingdom? Ohmigod, do you run an underage brothel?'

'Mia!' For the first time since he walked through the door of my ruined house and into my mess of a life, Sebastian looked flustered.

As we sat in the car, and I waited patiently for a worthy explanation, the front doors opened and a stream of girls burst through. They were dressed head to foot in tight-fitting grey jumpsuits with long poles strapped across their backs. Like water breaking around a boulder in a stream, they swarmed past the car and sprinted off across the open lawn to the right of where we were parked.

A tall, lithe student with long red hair split from the group and began shouting commands. The others quickly manoeuvred into pairs and began sweeping their arms in slow, deliberate movements.

'Are they dancing?'

Sebastian shook his head and reached for the door handle.

'They are training, using Tai Chi movements to prepare their bodies ahead of the hand-to-hand combat.'

'Hand-to-hand combat! What the hell is hand-to...?'

I didn't get a chance to finish my sentence as the girls swung the poles off their backs and began fighting each other, using them as weapons. The clash of wood on wood filled the early morning air as I stepped out of the car.

They moved with grace and determination, and I was transfixed at how fast they could wield the long staffs. There were a few grunts and yelps as fingers got caught in the onslaught, but none of them gave up.

'This way, Mia. I want to get you settled into your room before breakfast.'

Reluctantly I followed Sebastian up the front steps, losing my footing as I kept an eye on the girls.

•• ● ••

I HAD TO admit, the interior entrance hall of Hood Academy was impressive. The high ceilings bore lavishly painted frescoes from Greek mythology. The walls were decorated in rich, golden, wood panelling that gleamed in the warm light cast from the chandeliers. Chunky pieces of furniture hugged the walls. Intricately carved sideboards, full of dusty old books and red sofas occupied every available space. The room was clearly designed to be multipurpose. An inviting entrance for visitors and a communal gathering space for the students. To the left, through an open door, I could see a large dining area. Several tables and long benches filled the floor space, and I heard the gentle clatter of cutlery being laid out.

Directly to my right a half-glazed door stood slightly ajar with a name plaque in the centre. Dr Sebastian Roberts.

So my uncle was a doctor; interesting.

Two staircases leading off from the hallway dominated the space; one veered to the left and the other to the right. Sebastian walked up the left-hand stairs and I followed, swinging my rucksack over one shoulder.

'Breakfast will be served at eight in the dining room. Follow the smell and you should be fine. If you need me, come to my office, anytime.'

'What is this place?'

Sebastian stopped suddenly on the stairs, and I walked straight into the back of him. Jumping back, I grabbed onto the handrail to steady myself.

'Mia, there is so much you don't know, so much that your dad probably should have told you but didn't. I need you to be open-minded about this place.'

When he looked at me, I noticed the dark circles under his eyes, and I allowed myself a brief moment of guilt. Was he grieving over the loss of his brother? In the horror of the aftermath, I hadn't considered it, or maybe I just didn't care enough.

He turned his back and kept on walking up the stairs. It seemed that neither of us could communicate our true feelings.

We stopped on the first-floor landing and Sebastian gestured to the higher levels.

'The second and third floors are for the older students and teachers. This floor is for our newest students. We do maintain a basic curriculum of maths, English and science, but predominantly your studies will be centred around learning to fight, defend yourself and hunt.'

My mouth went dry, and all I could hear was the sound of a clock ticking somewhere off in the distance.

'What exactly is it that I'm learning to hunt?' I said, deliberately grinding out each word.

'Werewolves, Mia. You will be hunting werewolves.'

I SAT ON the end of the bed and stared at the wall. He had been so matter-of-fact when he'd told me. So cold and clinical. Not once did he stop to think that I might not believe him or that I'd laugh in his face and tell him there was no such thing.

Memories of a huge brown wolf crashing through our living room window stomped through my thoughts. I'd seen it with my own eyes. Fear had crippled me as I watched the creature pace the floor, broken glass crunching beneath its immense paws. The only other sound had been the whimpering sobs from my dad. He didn't move to protect me, he just mumbled words I couldn't understand. And then, the creature launched itself forward to rip my dad's throat out. As it turned to face me, all I could focus on were the hazel eyes and blood, lots and lots of blood, smeared over a long snout, and sharp fangs.

I stood up and paced the floor.

Sebastian had dropped his bombshell, dumped me in my new room and left. He had nothing more to say to me. Did he know what I'd seen? Was he fully aware that a werewolf had killed his brother?

My head was spinning as I tried to comprehend everything that had happened. In twelve short hours, I'd watched a mythical creature murder my dad, been whisked away by an estranged uncle werewolf hunter and had an odd conversation about my brother with a complete stranger.

I'd just hung my coat on the hook behind the door when it burst open and a pretty, young blonde girl dashed inside and collided with me. We both fell and hit the floor with a bang.

'Oh no, I'm so sorry. Are you okay?' She jumped to her feet, extending her hand to help me up. 'I didn't know you'd arrived.'

'I didn't know you were expecting me.' I fumbled to my feet with her help and dusted off my jeans.

'You're Mia, Dr Roberts's niece. He told us you were joining the school and I, for one, am so excited to be your roomie.'

I glanced around the bedroom, seeing it properly for the first time. There were single beds on either side of the room with a large mahogany dressing table separating them. Single wardrobes and a huge chest of drawers sat on the opposite wall. A doorway led to a private bathroom. Fresh cream linen and soft blankets covered the bed I'd been sitting on, whereas the other bed was covered in multicoloured cushions and an assortment of stuffed animals. Rich purple curtains framed the window and a plush grey rug stretched across the centre of the room.

'I'm Elizabeth, but my friends call me Lizzie.'

I shrugged and sat back on the bed, crossing my legs underneath me.

'I guess you know all about me, then.'

Unfazed by my abrupt manner, Elizabeth sat on the end of her bed and scrutinised me.

'You look so similar to your mum.'

I recoiled.

'How the hell do you know what my mum looks like?'

'Oh, there are tons of photographs in Dr R's office. When I first arrived here, I thought the pictures were of his wife. I actually told him I thought his wife was pretty.' She laughed and her blue eyes twinkled.

'What did he say?'

'He got all embarrassed and told me she was his sister-in-law but that they were close. I felt like such an idiot.'

Her smile was infectious, and I could feel the corners of my mouth twitching in an attempt to return her warmth. She was nice. I didn't know how to handle nice. So I did what I do best and clamped down on any attempt at being friendly.

'Have you eaten? Breakfast is great and there's plenty of it. Come on.'

My stomach growled, confirming that I hadn't eaten for far too long. Elizabeth giggled, and grabbing my hand she pulled me off the bed and towards the door.

She ignored my veiled attempts at being moody and didn't stop talking all the way to the dining hall, filling me in on which student stayed in which room, who held the best parties and where to get my equipment. As we got to the ground floor, I noticed another door close to Sebastian's office. I hadn't seen it when I first arrived.

'Where does that lead?'

Elizabeth pondered the existence of the door for a moment then shrugged her delicate shoulders.

'I think it's Dr R's storeroom. It's always locked and I don't remember ever seeing anyone use it.'

I followed Elizabeth into the dining hall. The smell of bacon and eggs filled the air and I realised just how hungry I was.

With a full plate and a large mug of hot chocolate, I trailed behind Elizabeth to sit at one end of the dining table. The hall was full of students, in their grey jumpsuits, chatting and eating and laughing. It was strange to think this was a school. The lunch hall back at my old school hadn't been as upbeat. In fact, nobody dared to eat the slop they dished up or to take on the *popular* kids who taunted anyone with a pulse.

I was halfway through my sausages when a hush fell over the room. I glanced up to see the tall red-haired girl from the garden saunter into the hall with what looked like two bodyguards bringing up the rear. I rolled my eyes. Apparently even Hood Academy had its own *popular* crew.

Elizabeth stiffened beside me as I became aware of the redhead hovering over me.

'You must be Mia.'

I chewed the remains of my breakfast and swallowed before staring up at her stern face.

'Stay out of my way.'

With that, our introduction was over, and she left as quickly as she'd arrived. The hush lifted and the laughter resumed.

'Who the hell is she?'

Elizabeth glanced nervously around her.

'That's Felicity. She's a true breed.'

'A what?'

'True breed! Her father, grandmother and great-grandmother were all hunters. She's the latest in a long line of dedicated hunters. They've written books about her family.'

'Well, I don't give a crap about her ancestors or her inbreeding, she's a freak.'

Elizabeth sniggered. 'True breed not inbreed.'

'Whatever. I don't like her.'

'No-one does. Because of her family's connections, she gets to run some of our training sessions and pushes us to the limits, and it's hard for the younger kids.'

'How long have you been here?'

'I'm still in my first year. A werewolf attacked my sister and me when we were camping last summer, so my parents enrolled me here.'

'I don't get it. Why did your family ship you off and not your sister?'

'She doesn't have the sight. Only I could see the werewolf.'

'So you only get to be a hunter if you can see werewolves?'

'Yes, you can't fight something you can't see. When did you see your first werewolf?'

I closed my eyes and then thought better of it as the scene unfolded in my mind for the millionth time.

'Yesterday, when it jumped through our living room window and murdered my dad.'

THREE

lizabeth was right. Sebastian's office was full of old photographs, not just of my mum, but my dad too. I picked up a brass frame with a faded picture inside; three happy faces beamed up at me. I'd never seen my dad smile. Being so young when my mum died meant that I missed out on the pleasant side of family life.

Sebastian opened the door and stopped midway between his office and the hallway, his jaw slack and eyes wide.

'You did say I could come and see you anytime, remember?'

With a deep sigh, he walked into the office and closed the door behind him.

'Sorry, Mia, I'm still getting used to seeing your face.'

'Oh, thanks. I see we both need to work on our family bonding skills.'

I flopped into one of the armchairs that sat in front of his desk, tracing the intricate carvings with my fingertips.

'You've got a lot of old stuff in this house.'

He huffed and I realised that was as close as he came to a laugh.

'The original owner of the property left the house and its contents to me in their will. I've just added the odd piece over the years.'

I stood up and walked across to the large picture window. The view looked out over the front lawns, the same piece of land where I'd watched a bunch of schoolgirls thrash the living hell out of one another.

'I can't do this.' I watched as it started to rain, big fat blobs of water chasing each other along the imperfections of the glass. 'Actually, scrap that. I don't *want* to do this.'

I spun around to catch him studying me from his leather desk chair, his fingers laced together behind his perfectly coiffed head of hair.

'I understand now why you brought me here, but I don't know why I could see that werewolf. I do know that I don't want to get that close and personal with another one anytime soon.'

He lowered his arms and placed his large hands flat on the desk. He addressed his knuckles when he finally spoke.

'Why didn't it kill you, Mia?'

'What?'

'How is it that you survived a werewolf attack that claimed the life of your father?'

I opened my mouth to speak, but the words dried up in my throat. I'd asked myself that same question over and over. The sight of all that blood, the broken glass and the piercing scream as the creature's fangs ripped out my dad's throat. Those huge brown eyes that looked...sad. It had played out in my mind a million times. I was paralysed with fear, unable to move a muscle, and I thought I was going to be next to die. The wolf watched me for a long time as if it was studying my reaction. When it approached, terror had vibrated through my entire body, but it licked my hand and then left.

'Werewolves know when they are facing a hunter, Mia. That monster could see that you were dangerous and it fled.'

I shook my head. That wasn't right.

'No, it could have killed me, but it didn't. It just walked away.'

Sebastian rose from his chair and walked over to the nearest bookshelf. He pulled out an old book, bound in soft green leather, and handed it to me.

'The history of the hunter line is in this book. I suggest you read it before making any rash decision to dismiss your calling.'

'My calling! I don't have a calling, I'm a sixteen-year-old orphan with no friends, and I have severe trust issues.'

He huffed again.

'What about your roommate, Elizabeth? She's a pleasant young girl.'

'Oh, now I get it.' I threw my hands in the air. 'How much did you pay her to befriend me?'

'I didn't pay anyone, Mia. Have a little faith in people.'

'It's very hard to have faith when your own flesh and blood made your life a living hell.'

'What your father did to you was unforgivable. He can't change what he did, and he can't make it right, but I can. I can take his place and look after you.'

I had a highly inappropriate urge to giggle. It was clearly well out of Sebastian's comfort zone to act the all-conquering uncle, but here he was, pleading for me to stay put.

'Give it a try,' he said softly. 'If you're still unhappy here in a few months, I'll enrol you in the secondary school in town. You can go off and be a normal teenager and leave all this behind.' He swept his arm out in an arc.

'I'll do my best, but I'm not making any guarantees. I'll try to fit in with your weird hunters, but if this doesn't work I'll hold you to that promise of a normal life.'

The corner of his mouth twitched as he nodded.

'I promise, Mia. Now, let's go find your tutor. She's a lethal hunter and an excellent teacher, and I *do* have to pay her to be your friend.'

I laughed and followed him out of the office. Mysterious uncle had a sense of humour; maybe there was hope for this place yet.

•• • ● • ••

MISS ROSS SWEPT an analytical eye over me before piling two jumpsuits, a tracksuit and various other outfits into my arms. Topping the pile with a pair of dark grey pumps, she steered me out of the stock room and back to the staircase.

'Drop it all off in your room and then meet me back here. I want to give you the grand tour.' She beamed at me and nudged me gently towards the stairs.

None of my teachers back home had been so nice. They'd tried to help me, but I'd turned away from all of them. With nobody to talk to, and no friends to speak of, I was easy to forget, and so, after a while, they stopped checking up on me. I became a ghost.

Here, in such a short time, I'd potentially made a friend and engaged positively with a member of the teaching staff. There was a lightness about me that felt alien, but not at all unpleasant.

When I got back to the entrance hall, Miss Ross was waiting patiently for me. She led us out of the front door, and we deviated towards the side of the building, walking along the flower beds until we came to a low stone wall.

We stopped briefly, which allowed me a glance at the extensive grounds that spread out across the back of the property. Huge circular lawns divided by gravel paths and neatly trimmed shrubs stretched for miles around us.

'The building dates back to 1866,' said Miss Ross, sweeping a hand wide to encompass the Victorian architecture. 'The gardens were designed at the same time to complement the buildings.'

I glanced to the right of us where a large willow tree with a stone bench beneath its branches stood proudly. A

SHELLEY WILSON

young man tended to the borders nearby with a long-handled spade.

'That's Adam. He's the groundsman.'

Adam looked up at the mention of his name and gave us a wave.

We moved off and cut across the open lawns until we reached an old wall. The aged stones were discoloured and covered in overgrown ivy revealing the level of neglect on this part of the estate.

Beyond the wall lay a dirt track, leading down to what looked like outbuildings or a stable block.

There was a row of four cages with iron bars and heavy doors, all of them empty. The ceilings were far too low to accommodate a horse but were just high enough for a person to stand up if they curved their shoulders.

'What is this place?'

'Years ago, we used to catch the werewolves and hold them in the animal cages, but these days Sebastian prefers to keep any captives in alternative accommodation.'

'Captives? What do you mean?'

'Well, the creatures are only wolves at the full moon or if they are provoked by attack. The rest of the time they are as human as you and me. Sebastian thought it more humane to let the prisoners rest inside rather than on the ground outside.'

Shock reverberated through my bones, the image of those sad brown eyes flashing across my mind. Yes, the animal was terrifying, but imagining it in its human form was too much to take in.

'Come on, I want to show you the gymnasium next.' She bounded off up the track heading back to the academy, leaving me reeling at her revelation.

The wind picked up ever so slightly and ruffled my hair as I watched the lethal hunter bounce lightly up the path. I glanced back at the cages and swallowed down the nausea. A snap behind me made me jump, and I whirled around. There was nobody there, only the endless woods that bordered the property. I shook my head to dislodge the unease, certain that my mind must be playing tricks on me. The trees swayed gently as the wind lifted the leaves and shook them, the scent of damp earth and moss filling the air.

I backed away from the forest with a heavy heart. Would my hunter training keep me from enjoying the woods and nature? Was I destined to shed blood and cage these creatures? I'd told Sebastian I'd give him a couple of months and I would do my best to stand by that promise. But as I rushed past the animal cages I felt closer to despair than anything else.

•• ● ● ●••

'I WAS SORRY to hear about your father.' Miss Ross stepped in front of me and I forced myself to look up into her face. She was probably in her late fifties and still strikingly beautiful, her dark skin complemented by the bright blue jumper she wore.

Her voice echoed around the huge room with wooden floors and ropes suspended from the ceiling. She'd referred to it as the gym, but it looked more like an army assault course.

'Thank you. The police said they'd contact my uncle if they find anything out.'

She smiled at me, her gaze flickering to the fading bruise on my cheek. 'Mia, I want you to prepare yourself for the possibility that your father's death will be classed as a cold case. The investigators won't find anything because it was a supernatural death.'

She paused to fiddle with a stack of boxing mitts. 'What happened to your father is happening all over the world. It's our job, as hunters, to put a stop to these attacks. The murders remain unsolved as the police fail to find answers.'

Was it wrong to tell her that my father may have deserved what happened to him? He had been an evil monster too, no fangs or sharp claws, but what made him any different?

I didn't think my confession would help the situation, so I shut my mouth and nodded along as she explained the need for hunters and how the work they did was for the greater good.

When she started to talk about my mum, I snapped to attention.

'You knew her?'

'Yes, I knew her. She was a lovely lady, a very talented photographer and a welcome visitor to the academy. Your uncle was very close to her.'

'Yeah, I've seen the photos in his office. It was a bit creepy. Dad didn't even have any pictures of her at home.'

'Well, I'm sure her death was a huge blow to your father. Grief can cause ordinary people to do extraordinary things.'

'Was my mum a hunter too?'

The silence stretched out. A tiny muscle in Miss Ross's jaw worked hard as she formulated a response. I began to think I'd rather not know until finally she spoke.

'She was passionate about the work Sebastian was doing here, and she understood the importance of the hunters' oath, but no, she wasn't a hunter.'

'What's the hunters' oath?'

'Once you begin your full training you will be sworn in to the academy. It's a great honour to serve as a hunter, and we uphold that tradition by requesting that our students swear allegiance in front of their fellow students to be loyal and fierce.'

'If my mum wasn't a hunter, how did she know about the oath?'

'I believe your uncle explained the ceremony.'

By the tone of her voice, I knew that more questions weren't going to be welcome, and as she made her way to the exit, I realised that my tour was also at an end.

'We'll catch up tomorrow in class, Mia.'

Then she was gone, leaving me with a head full of questions and an ache in my heart.

•• • ● • ••

I ATE LUNCH alone, as the other students were in class. The silence was a welcome distraction. It was hard to take in some of the information I'd received since Sebastian had turned up at my house.

After devouring a burger and fries, I found my way back to the front entrance and ran up the stairs two at a time, eager to get back to my room.

Three figures blocked the way as I reached the corridor to the bedrooms. Felicity and her squad watched me as I made my way towards them.

'You don't belong here.' Felicity crossed her arms over her chest and swung her fiery hair over her shoulder.

'Why not?' I didn't really want to get involved in a war of words with the resident school bitch, but the look on Felicity's face told me I wasn't getting away from her anytime soon.

'Sebastian has worked incredibly hard to build this academy into a respected school for hunters, and the likes of you will lower the tone.'

'I wouldn't be here if I hadn't seen a werewolf, so I guess that makes me a hunter, and that means I am eligible to attend the academy.' I crossed my arms to mirror her standoffish body language.

She laughed loudly, a cruel sound that dripped with malice.

'You may have seen a werewolf, but you will never be a hunter. Sebastian knows it, I know it, and soon enough you'll realise it. When Sebastian rushed off to collect you, my father called your uncle and told him exactly what he thought about you coming here. You're not welcome. You are weak like your mother and a waste of space just like your father.'

Her smile was callous as she spun on her grey pumps and stalked off down the corridor. I felt winded. The lightness that I'd felt earlier left in a whoosh and a heavy rock settled on my chest, squeezing out any emotion I had managed to claw back.

Through a haze of tears, I ran back down the stairs and out through the front door. I didn't falter, sprinting across the open lawn, down the gravel driveway and into the woods beyond. I kept running and I didn't look back.

•• • ● • ••

THE AIR WAS crisp as I ventured deeper into the woods. I don't know how far I ran or how long I had been running but the further I went the more relaxed I became. Eventually, I stopped running and strolled through the trees at a more leisurely pace, noticing the fauna around me. When the sky began to darken and my stomach growled, I realised I must have missed dinner.

I kicked myself for not taking more notice of my surroundings; I was in a strange town and didn't know anyone, and yet being in the woods felt familiar and safe.

I remembered the times Zak had taken me to the park close to our house, which had a small pond. The neighbourhood boys had set up a tyre swing across the water and dared each other to swing across. I used to climb one of the trees and sit in its branches, watching the boys fall in the pond or cut their knees. They were happier times full of laughter and innocence.

I pushed through the drooping branches of a willow tree and stopped. Beyond the trees was an outcropping of rocks; big boulders bleached a sandy colour by the sun were now illuminated by the light of the moon. I climbed the nearest rock, its surface smooth and cool to the touch. Swinging my legs over the edge, I marvelled at the view.

Far below, the countryside stretched out like a blanket. On the horizon, I could make out the twinkling lights of Ravenshood, the town Sebastian had driven through on our way to the academy.

I watched the world ready itself for the evening, and a sense of peace settled over me. A cool breeze ruffled my hair, and I wished I'd grabbed a jumper as I ran away. I was pondering how I would find my way back to the academy when a sharp noise in the bushes behind me made me jump.

Shit.

Standing up, I backed away from the edge, keeping an eye on the surrounding bushes and trees. The moon was large and bright in the sky, bathing the woods in a creamy iridescent glow.

Double shit.

Looking up through the overhanging branches, I watched the wisps of grey cloud float across the moon, momentarily hiding it from view. Last night the moon had been at its fullest, and as Miss Ross told me only hours earlier, werewolves changed on the full moon. Did she mean for just one night, or did they stay in their wolf form for a few nights?

Shit, shit, shit.

The bushes ahead of me stirred. My heart hammered inside my chest. I strained to see what was in the bushes. My palms were sticky and a bead of sweat trickled down my spine. Whatever it was, it was getting closer. I backed up to the nearest tree and felt the bark dig into my shoulders. The bush parted and a wild rabbit hopped forward, sniffing the ground as it searched for food.

I let out a deep breath and leant my head back against the tree trunk, my shoulders sagging against the rough bark.

All the talk of werewolves and hunters had me spooked, and I was turning into a quivering mess. The rabbit was oblivious to my distress and continued foraging for its dinner as

I pushed away from the tree and turned in the direction of the academy.

My heart froze and my legs trembled as I came face-to-face with four sets of eyes. The huge wolves were standing in a semicircle just ahead of me. Their eyes gleamed in the moonlight, and the fur on their hides shimmered under the bulbous moon. They were immense, much larger than any of the wolves I'd seen on *Animal Planet*.

A brown wolf, this one even bigger than the rest, separated from the pack and took a tentative step forward, sniffing the air.

My dad's screams echoed in my head as the other wolves followed and circled me. The terror I felt held me in its rigid grip; the only part of me I could move were my eyes. I wanted to close them, squeeze them shut so I didn't see the blow when it came, but whether it was morbid curiosity or something else, I couldn't stop watching them.

They walked around me, never looking away. Sebastian had said the wolf that killed my dad knew I was a hunter. If these wolves had any suspicion that I could be dangerous, they weren't showing it. In fact, they probably knew I was a hunter-in-training and would snuff me out before my first lesson.

My legs were shaking as I struggled to stay upright. Every inch of my being wanted to lie down and curl up into a tight ball.

The brown wolf growled, and I braced myself for the attack, but instead of launching itself in a flash of fangs it turned its back and walked away. Two others followed, and I watched them disappear into the darkness of the trees. The last wolf was much paler than the others, the light of the moon reflecting off its golden fur. I was drawn in by its blue eyes, which sparkled like the ocean. It hung its head to one side, and I got the distinct impression that it was giving me a lopsided smirk. I blinked and it spun away, bounding off into the woods.

It was a good twenty minutes until I could move any of my limbs. For a short moment, I thought it had started raining but then I realised I was crying. Whether that was from fear, relief or a mixture of the two, I wasn't sure. This was the second time in as many days that I had escaped death or at the very least serious injury. I was too numb to process what that might mean, but I knew I couldn't chance the wolves returning to finish me off. Eventually, the feeling in my legs returned and I stumbled through the trees, slowly at first and then picking up speed until I was sprinting through the woods and hoping it was in the direction of the academy.

SHELLEY WILSON

FOUR

I hadn't realised I was still holding my breath until I spotted the glaring lights of the school in the distance and I released a loud sob. As the woods petered out and the lawn came into view, I raced the rest of the way.

Sebastian was waiting for me on the front steps when I approached the old building. His face was a mixture of anger and relief.

'Where did you go?'

'I needed some fresh air so I went for a walk in the woods.' I leapt up the stairs until I stood in front of him and then stopped, folding my arms protectively across my chest. If he had even a sliver of my dad's temper, I was in for a barrage of abuse.

It was clear to anyone that I had been crying, but he either didn't notice or he chose to ignore it. The dark cloud that crossed his face lifted temporarily as he let out a long, slow breath as if he'd been holding it in for hours.

'I have dealt with Felicity. She was bragging about her treatment of you to some of the girls in the common room and Miss Ross overheard.'

I cringed. If she had received a roasting because I'd skipped out, I was certain there would be repercussions. If not from Felicity, then from her girlie goons.

'There was no need for that,' I said. 'She's a bitch and doesn't know how to behave in any other way. I can handle her.'

'I don't want you to have to handle her. She can be passionate about the academy, and it doesn't always come across in the right way.'

'Passionate! Oh, she's definitely passionate, especially when it comes to her hatred towards my parents. What the hell's that about?'

Sebastian sucked a breath in sharply.

'I want you to ignore her and keep out of her way. Her family are wealthy benefactors for the academy, and she believes this gives her a right to interfere in how I manage the school. Clearly she is a young girl out of her depth.'

'She's an idiot, and I'm more than happy to stay out of her way. Is that all?'

Sebastian studied me for a while longer before nodding. If he had any inclination that I'd had a run-in with wolves, he wasn't letting on.

'Yes, get some sleep, I know Elizabeth was worried about you, so she'll be glad to see you're back safe.'

I smiled to myself as I walked through the front door. It felt nice to know that someone cared.

'Mia.'

I looked back over my shoulder. Sebastian was standing with his back to me, looking out over the grounds and into the woods.

'I don't want you to take a walk in the forest at night again. Do you understand?'

He couldn't see me nodding as he was still staring at the trees, but I knew that walking in the woods at night wouldn't be on my to-do list any more.

'Sure, whatever. Goodnight, Sebastian.'

'Goodnight, Mia.'

•• ● ••

THE LAMP WAS on in the bedroom when I crept through the door. I had thought that Elizabeth would be sitting up waiting for me after what Sebastian said, but the long wait had clearly exhausted her. She was fully clothed and propped up on her pillows, fast asleep and surrounded by masses of stuffed animals. She looked incredibly young as I checked her sleeping form, but she was the same age as me. Maybe the dark circles under my eyes were a side effect of a lousy life.

I slipped into my sleep shorts and T-shirt and climbed between the clean sheets. The bed was soft and comfortable, and I was suddenly aware of my aching limbs. Running wasn't an everyday occurrence for me, especially at the breakneck speed I'd fled the woods. My mind wandered back to the wolves. Despite Sebastian's warnings, the animals hadn't attacked. Did they believe I was a hunter and could destroy them? Somehow I didn't think so. There had to be another reason I had been spared—twice—and I intended to find out why. Sebastian's office was the best place to start. Tomorrow. First, I needed to get a good night's sleep.

There was a light tap at the window and then another. Something struck the glass. Elizabeth stirred and I was just about to open my mouth to warn her to be quiet when a male voice called her name. Elizabeth's eyes flew open and she grinned at me in the pale moonlight streaming through the curtains.

'It's Adam,' she whispered, bouncing off the bed.

'The groundsman?' I recalled the handsome, dark-skinned gardener I'd seen during my tour of the grounds earlier.

She nodded enthusiastically and climbed on the desk. I raised an eyebrow as she unlocked the window latch.

'We're two floors up,' I hissed. I knew I was stating the obvious but I worried that in her euphoria Elizabeth had forgotten this simple fact and would launch herself into mid-air.

She giggled. 'I know, silly.'

There was a light tap and the top of a ladder appeared against the frame as Adam's face appeared at the window.

'Come inside, quickly.' Elizabeth grabbed his arms to help steady him.

With his dark skin and black clothing, Adam was perfectly camouflaged against the night sky. He swung his long legs over the sill and jumped down to the floor.

Elizabeth laced her fingers through his and glanced in my direction. Her expression was one of delight and also apprehension. Was she worried that I'd disapprove?

'Mia, I'd like you to officially meet Adam.'

I climbed out of bed and extended my hand to the handsome young man who fidgeted on the spot.

'It's lovely to meet you.'

Adam's posture relaxed as he took my hand and shook it. His palms were rough to the touch, no doubt from working in the academy garden, but his smile was genuine and I found myself warming to him.

'It's great to meet you in person, Mia.'

Elizabeth grinned at me and bounced up and down on the balls of her feet.

'I'm so sorry I didn't tell you about him sooner, but with everything that's been going on I didn't get a chance, and then you weren't at dinner and...'

I put my hand up to stop her chattering.

'It's fine, really. You don't need to tell me your business.'

'Oh, but I do; we're friends and roomies. We must share our deepest secrets.' She turned to smile up at Adam, then added, 'And he's mine.'

SHELLEY WILSON

I suddenly felt the urge to flee. Soppy looks and romantic gestures were for romance novels and chick flicks and I didn't have the first clue how to *be* around that.

'I'm going for a walk,' I said, rather too loudly. 'I'll give you guys some privacy.'

I slipped my feet into my grey pumps, grabbed a hoodie and the small book Sebastian had given me and headed for the door.

'You don't have to leave, Mia.' Elizabeth's brow creased as she watched my fumbled attempt at escape.

'I know,' I said, smiling at my roommate, 'but I fancy exploring and hopefully I'll be able to avoid a certain redhead at this time of night.'

'Be careful,' she said.

·· • ● • ··

I DIDN'T WANT to think about the teenage romance that was unfolding back in my room. No matter what Elizabeth said, it was her business and nothing to do with me. I was, however, pleased that Adam seemed to be a decent lad. The boys back home had been cruel and relentless in their bullying. Zak had taught me at a young age who to avoid and how. A tip I should remember when trying to stay out of Felicity's way.

The redhead pushed her way into my thoughts as I crept along the first-floor corridor towards the staircase. Why did Felicity hate me so much? Why did I care? It wasn't that I wanted us to bond and braid each other's hair but she possessed a deep-set vindictiveness that involved my entire family and that bothered me.

There was no-one around at this time of night. Sebastian's office door was closed and no light shone through the glass to indicate he was up and still working. I realised I didn't even know where his bedroom was. He had failed to share that with me. Clearly I only had access to him during office hours.

The cafeteria was in darkness and the heavy wooden doors that I'd sprinted out of earlier today were now shut and bolted. I curled up on one of the many sofas hugging the wall in the entrance hall, flicked on a small table lamp and pulled out the green leather book Sebastian had given me.

The pages were well worn and yellowed, their edges marked in gold. A handwritten inscription on the first page read: *'Never stop searching, love C x.'* I recognised the handwriting instantly from the rescued pages of my mum's poetry, and my pulse quickened as I thought about my mum, Cassie Roberts. This message was from her. I raised an eyebrow as I turned the book over in my hand, searching for some other message sent from beyond the grave. The book had come from Sebastian's bookshelf, and judging by the number of photographs of my mum in his office, they obviously had a deeper connection than anyone realised.

The book covered every topic from the history of hunters to weaponry through the ages. It was the strapline on the title page that caught my eye.

To every pack, a cub is born.

Unleash the hunter to protect and serve.

The author, a man named Dr P.S. Neale, had written a long-winded introduction, dated 1862. He waffled on about the importance of hunters and how they were necessary to correct the balance of nature, of creatures so vile and brutal that Queen Victoria herself had assigned him as a master hunter to the realm.

Impressive. Not only was I now a member of an elite werewolf hunting academy, but apparently we were to report directly to the royal family.

According to Dr Neale, it was the birth of a child to a werewolf mother that triggered the hunter gene in a human child. Mother Nature's way of balancing good and evil. For every werewolf that gave birth to a cub, a hunter was born to kill it.

Closing the book, I rested my head back against the wall. Did I believe that all this supernatural crap was true? Sebastian believed in it. He ran a school dedicated to that principle. I certainly couldn't deny that werewolves existed, but hunters being born for the sole purpose of killing them? I wasn't so sure about that. Besides, there were hundreds of girls in Hood Academy. Surely there weren't hundreds of werewolves hiding in the surrounding woods.

From somewhere upstairs I heard hushed voices and the sound of people approaching. I switched off the light and slid off the sofa to crouch on the floor, hiding myself away behind a large mahogany dresser.

Felicity's voice was clear and harsh. 'It's a privilege to see what I'm about to show you. Nobody else in this godawful school even knows about the lab.'

The two girls walked across the foyer oblivious to my presence and headed for the door beside Sebastian's office. It was the one I'd seen yesterday, the one Elizabeth had thought was a store room. From the pocket of her jeans, Felicity produced a key and quietly unlocked the door, swinging it open. She glanced around the dark foyer and I crouched lower, curling myself up so as not to be seen.

Satisfied that they were alone, Felicity ushered her companion inside.

I raced across the carpet, catching the handle so the door couldn't click shut behind them. A torch light bounced off the walls, and I waited until their muffled voices had faded away before following.

The small space looked like a typical store room until I moved further in. Shelves covered the walls from floor to ceiling with stacks of paper, printer inks and dusty exercise books, but beyond the shelves was a long corridor hidden from view behind the shelving unit. A faint light glowed in the distance, and I could see shadows moving about. Felicity and her companion disappeared through an opening to the right.

My heartbeat was rapid as I tiptoed after the two girls. Maybe this was an unknown route to the science classrooms. Somehow I didn't think that was true. The same feeling of dread I felt earlier, coming face-to-face with the wolves, trickled back into my veins.

A low moan filled the darkness and I dropped to my knees. It didn't sound like Felicity or her companion. The sound was masculine. The moaning ceased and I was about to creep forward when a scream filled the air. The hairs on the back of my neck rose at the desperate sound. I was close to the entrance where the girls had disappeared. Hugging the wall, I skulked closer until I was alongside the opening. I risked a quick look around the corner and saw that it opened up onto a staircase that went to a lower floor. The screams were coming from below.

Felicity's wild laughter floated up the staircase.

Although they were faint, I could hear her words clearly.

'Do it again. That's right, hold the knife in your right hand and press down. Don't worry, nobody in the school can hear us. The lab is soundproofed.' A dreadful howl followed, and I felt bile rise up in my throat. Whatever they were doing down there, it wasn't good.

'You deserve to die.' Felicity's voice filled the darkness and her friend laughed.

I spun on my heel and ran. The entrance hall was still empty when I emerged from the store room. Nobody heard those terrible screams because the rooms were secure. Did that mean Sebastian knew about the lab, or the prisoner? I knew that I should run and tell my uncle what I'd heard, but my gut instinct told me not to trust him. Not yet. I pushed the door closed behind me and rushed to the stairs, taking them two at a time. I needed to get back to my room. I wanted to feel safe, but I doubted that I'd ever feel that way again.

FIVE

The morning sky was overcast as the student body filed through the huge wooden doors and assembled on the front lawn. Miss Ross stood on the top steps surveying the bleary-eyed girls like a kestrel watching its prey. I spotted Felicity and her squad congregating by a tall flagpole stuck in the grass and steered Elizabeth to a stop at the furthest possible point from them.

'Avoidance tactics,' I mumbled when Elizabeth gave me a quizzical look.

When I returned to our bedroom last night Adam had left and my roommate was fast asleep. Something I was grateful for. I wasn't sure if I could, or should, confide in Elizabeth about what I'd seen and heard in the secret store room. I didn't want to get her mixed up in any trouble.

Miss Ross punctured my thoughts as she called for silence.

'Today's assignment is our boot-camp training run,' she said.

A rumble of discord filled the air.

'Yes, yes, I know how much you love these runs, but our stamina, strength and agility are what make us deadly. The only way to maintain the high level of fitness that Hood Academy is famous for is to push ourselves to the limit.'

'What's a boot-camp training run?' I asked Elizabeth who was stretching her calf muscles out.

'We've got to run through the woods, loop around the town and return before dark.'

'Doesn't sound so bad. Why does everyone look like she just cancelled Christmas?'

'It's about fifty miles.'

'Whoa, fifty! That's really far. How often do you do this?'

'We run regular circuits once a week but Miss Ross likes to spring the ultra-marathon on us at least twice a year.'

'Terrific,' I mumbled, grabbing my ankle and bending my leg back in a vague attempt to warm up my quads. 'There's no way I'll be back before dark. Do they send out search parties?'

Elizabeth laughed. 'The route is marked with green flags. Just follow them and you'll be fine. If you're not back at the academy by nine, Miss Ross collects the stragglers in the minibus.'

'Well, that's a relief. Maybe I could just take a book with me and lounge around at the final marker until it gets dark.'

'I'll run with you and we'll take it slow.' Elizabeth beamed at me and my mouth tugged in something resembling a smile of gratitude. She was really sweet and so far hadn't given up on me. Maybe I wasn't so unlovable after all.

•• • ● • ••

MISS ROSS WAS now standing next to the tall flagpole with a whistle in her hand. The students spread out across the lawn in varying degrees of panic. There were the ultra-sporty girls bouncing on their heels as they eagerly awaited the shrill screech of the start whistle, and then there were the rest of us. The *I can't believe we have to do this* brigade, loitering near the back.

'Remember to follow the markers, girls. The green flags are there to keep you safe and protected. We can't venture into unmapped territory, and I wouldn't want anyone to risk their lives for a training exercise.'

I spun to look at Elizabeth who quickly held her hand up as if expecting me to have something to say about this latest revelation.

'It's just a precaution,' she said. 'There are huge parts of the forest that even the tutors don't know about. Just stick to the path that's marked. No need to panic.'

'Panic! Who's panicking? It's my second day at this place and so far I've risked my life three times...' Elizabeth's eyebrow rose. 'Well, you've tasted the food here!'

She chuckled and I released the breath I'd been holding. It wasn't the right time to reveal my extracurricular activities or my run-in with the local werewolf pack.

The whistle sounded and everyone swarmed forward, jostling for elbow room. Miss Ross nodded at me as I passed her, giving me a pity thumbs up. She knew I wouldn't be able to breathe after the first mile. Maybe that thumbs up was her way of telling me she'd meet me soon with the minibus.

·· • ● • ··

ELIZABETH WAS CLEARLY using all her energy to stop herself from running at a half-decent pace and I felt a pang of guilt.

'You should go ahead,' I rasped, already struggling to talk let alone suck air into my lungs. 'I'm fine, honestly. I'll meet you for dinner.'

'It's okay,' she said. 'I promised to look after you on this run.'

'Lizzie, I insist. You can look after my blisters when I get home later.'

She giggled. 'If you're sure.'

'Hundred per cent, now go.'

She gave me a sympathetic wave then shot off up the path, overtaking the other girls who were also striving to survive this physical assault Miss Ross had forced on us.

As I rasped my way further along the path the hairs on the back of my neck prickled, and I turned to look behind me, half expecting to see a few stragglers, but I could no longer see any of my fellow students. Even the most unfit girl in the school had overtaken me and disappeared into the trees. I was alone once more, and yet I had the strangest sensation that I was being watched.

I slowed down to a fast walking pace and wiped the sweat off my face with the bottom of my T-shirt. The sound of the birds high up in the branches filled the air, and I could hear the distant trickle of a stream. My breathing steadied, and I felt a deep sense of belonging. Zak would love it here. The small dell back home had been our sanctuary but these woods, with their endless paths and beautiful clearings, would have kept us amused for days at a time.

The path ahead split in two directions; the western route seemed to be the more obvious track as I knew the town was that way, but the green flag stood further along the eastern path.

I veered right and picked up the pace again heading away from town. The further I ran, the more uneven the path became. The compacted earth of the running track had given way to moss and weeds. Tree branches dangled across the trail making it difficult to run without bending to avoid a twig in the eye. There hadn't been a green flag for about half an hour, and I worried that I'd somehow missed a turning.

Sweeping aside a beautiful willow tree, I stepped into a clearing and froze. I knew this place. The same sandy-coloured rocks hugged the edge of the overhang where I'd marvelled at the view under a full moon.

Shit.

SHELLEY WILSON

My heart began to race as I looked around the clearing. Not twenty-four hours ago, I'd stood here, face-to-face with four huge wolves. How could Miss Ross lead her students through woods that the enemy had claimed? My mind wandered to the uneven path and the lack of green flags.

'Felicity.' I said her name aloud as if looking for confirmation from the trees that she had something to do with this. It had to be her. She was the kind of person who would change the flags and send me into danger. But I didn't feel like my life was in danger. In fact, I felt calm and comfortable. Finding this place again was like discovering silence in a storm.

There was no full moon to unnerve me this time, so I climbed onto the smooth rocks and took in the view. Fields, wooded glens and paddocks of grazing horses stretched out below me.

'Beautiful, isn't it?'

I jumped at the sound of a voice behind me. Scurrying to my feet, I half expected to find Elizabeth or Miss Ross. Instead, I was looking into the bluest eyes I'd ever seen.

A boy stood in the clearing, his hands shoved deep into his jeans pockets. His hair shone like brass despite the cloudy sky. He couldn't have been much older than me, perhaps seventeen.

'Sorry, I didn't mean to startle you. I'm Cody.' He gave me a lopsided smile.

'Mia.' I lifted my hand in a lame half wave.

'Can I sit with you?' He motioned to the overhang and I jumped back, giving him room to manoeuvre.

He walked to the edge of the rocks and lowered himself down, his long legs disappearing over the ledge, the lightly tanned flush to his skin deepening as he glanced back at me.

I hesitated for a moment before joining him, making sure I was a safe distance away.

'I love it here,' he whispered. 'It's always so quiet.'

'Why would you need to find a quiet spot?' I asked, wondering if he attended a boys' version of the academy.

'My family can get a bit loud so I like to escape.' His smile lit up his entire face, and I couldn't help but smile along with him.

'Do you have a large family?'

'My parents are foster carers and over the years we've grown as a family.' He laughed out loud. 'At the moment, I've got four brothers and two sisters.'

'Wow, that is...loud!'

He laughed again and I felt my shoulders relax with every second that passed.

'Your parents must be amazing,' I said.

'They were,' he replied softly. Unfortunately they were killed a few years ago.'

I mentally kicked myself.

'I'm so sorry. How did it happen?' I scolded myself a second time for asking such a personal question. It was none of my damn business, but I felt a strange bond with this boy. We were both orphans who had been touched by tragedy and looking for an escape.

Cody didn't seem to notice my discomfort.

'It was a car accident. They were here one minute and gone the next. My brothers have looked after me ever since it happened.'

'I'm sorry to hear that. My mum was killed in a hit-and-run, so I understand that pain, but it sounds like your parents did a wonderful job of raising all those kids, if they're still here for you when you need them.'

I didn't mean to sound so envious, but it slipped out in my tone. Cody must have noticed as his eyebrows lifted slightly as he looked over at me.

I didn't want him asking about my tragic past, so I jumped in with another question.

'Do you live in the woods?'

He nodded, his fair hair flopping into his eyes.

'We live in a farmhouse deep in the woods. Luckily there's a lane that leads us to the outskirts of town so we're not totally cut off. My parents ran a vegetable store and sold all the produce they grew in the fields. We've kept it running ever since they died.'

'You don't look like a farmer.'

He laughed again and the sound melted something inside my chest.

'What do I look like?'

I could feel my face burning as I thought about an appropriate answer.

'You know, don't answer that. I don't think I want to know.' He smiled and tilted his head to the side. 'Want to see something cool?'

I grinned and he took that as a yes.

We left the outcrop and ventured further into the woods. Somewhere deep inside my subconscious I knew I shouldn't be wandering through the forest with a strange boy, but my gut told me a different story. I had the oddest sensation that I knew him—on an emotional level. We'd suffered the same tragedy and our grief united us.

The smell of the earth and woods filled my senses and calmed my nerves the further we walked. The trees began to thin out as we reached a clearing with a huge oak tree in the middle. It was like no tree I'd ever come across. The trunk was immense and someone had chiselled a seat into the wood.

'My dad carved this for me when I was little. I used to come here after they died so I could feel close to them again. This tree and the overhang are special places.'

I could understand that. After my mum died, I would sit in the bottom of her wardrobe soaking up the scent of her clothes and the lingering smell of her perfume. Loss is hard, but when you are so young it is life-altering.

'It's also a great climbing tree.'

He winked at me, extending an unspoken challenge, and strode off across the clearing until he stood beneath its branches. He reached up and grasped the lower bough, then swung one of his long legs up and over until he was perched in the tree.

'Come on up.' His voice was teasing as he began to swing higher and higher.

I hadn't climbed a tree in years, not since the days when Zak had taken me to the park as a kid. It came back to me in a rush of adrenalin and I scrambled up the branches, catching up to Cody in no time.

'Ah, an expert in tree climbing, I see. What other talents does the mysterious Mia hide beneath her grace and beauty?'

I couldn't stop myself from laughing. He had a way of making it feel easy.

My T-shirt clung to my back as I moved from branch to branch. I knew I looked like someone had thrown me in an oven and finished me off in the swimming pool, my mediocre run through the forest adding to my not-so-glamorous appearance. Cody, however, didn't seem bothered by my frizzy hair and blotchy cheeks. By the time we reached the top I was wheezing, but I felt fearless. Cody nestled into the crook of two branches and I did the same, our feet planted side by side.

'I can understand why you like coming here,' I said, trying to catch my breath.

Through the top layer of leaves we could see for miles. The houses and shops down in the valley glinted in the sunshine and the faint outline of the peaks framed the horizon. It was a breathtaking view.

We talked, mostly about our likes and dislikes, favourite music and authors. It was nice. Apart from with Elizabeth, I'd never really experienced the joy of a normal conversation without there being an ulterior motive. My dad always managed to twist my words, leaving me with an incessant fear of saying the wrong thing. His way of picking a fight. However, Cody was easy to talk to, and I was about to tell him this when he spoke up.

'So then, Mia, are you going to tell me what you were running from?'

I flinched slightly as suspicion flooded my senses. Had I misjudged my bad boy radar? I didn't think so. Cody didn't give off that homicidal maniac vibe, but how did he know I'd been running? Had he followed me to the outcrop? Realising that I'd done nothing wrong and was merely on a training exercise, I relaxed my shoulders.

We stared at each other across the branches of the tree. My mind whirled with possible scenarios that I could share without divulging too much. I opted for part truth in the hope that it would pacify his curiosity and spare me from the fear I felt at opening up.

'My dad recently passed away and my uncle brought me to live with him. He has this strange opinion that family should stick together.' I laughed, nervously.

Cody's head automatically dropped to the side in the universal language of sorrow and I glanced away. I didn't want to see the pity shining in his beautiful blue eyes. I omitted to tell him the part about the werewolves and the gore. It seemed safer sticking mainly to school-related topics, so instead I told him about my new life amongst the spawn of Satan, who happened to have red hair and her own set of bodyguards.

'Felicity and her crew are determined to make my life a living hell, but all I want to do is melt into the background and get on with my studies.'

'Are you talking about Hood Academy?'

'Yeah, I arrived yesterday, and I've already run away twice; doesn't bode well, does it?'

He smiled but his features were tight, not the open, warm expression from earlier.

'Is something wrong?' I asked.

'I've heard things about that school—bad things.'

'What kind of things?' I was starting to feel uneasy. Cody didn't seem to be talking about schoolgirl bullies. Did he know about the werewolf hunters? Could I ask him? I only realised at that moment that the academy might be a secret society, and here I was telling the first guy I stumbled across.

'I think I better go,' he muttered.

He began climbing down the tree, slowly at first and then much faster. I struggled to keep up and worried that he would run off and leave me. I didn't play the damsel-in-distress card very often, but I was lost in the woods and I kind of needed him to guide me back in the direction of the school.

I sat on the lowest branch and steadied myself to jump, but Cody raised his arms to help me down, and as I leapt he caught me.

His hands felt solid at my waist, and our bodies were so close I could smell the tang of his shower gel. I looked up into his bright eyes and saw a flickering of pain there.

'Follow the trail to the right and it will lead you back to the academy. Stick to the path and you shouldn't get lost again.'

'I feel like Dorothy in *The Wizard of Oz*,' I said quietly, trying to lighten the tension that was evident on his face and in the tightness of his hold.

He smiled, a fraction of that warmth returning to his eyes. If I had given some serious thought to the situation I would have said that Cody looked scared.

'Stay safe, Mia, and be careful who you trust.'

With that, he turned away and jogged off into the woods, leaving me reeling from his words and his touch.

•• • ● • ••

BEING THE FIRST to return back from the ultra-marathon should have been a memorable occasion. However, as I strolled across the lawn I could just make out Miss Ross's outline through Sebastian's office window. She threw her hands in the air and disappeared from view, only to reappear with

Sebastian by her side at the main door, rushing down the front steps of the academy and heading my way.

'What's wrong?' It was Sebastian who spoke first, worry etched in the frown lines across his forehead.

'Nothing. I got totally lost when I missed a green flag, but I managed to find my way back.'

I'd been proud of myself for following Cody's vague directions but the look of horror on Sebastian's face made me wish I'd stayed lost for a few more hours.

Miss Ross waved him away and herded me towards the school, wrapping her arm around my shoulder like a protective mother hen.

'You appear to have an aptitude for getting lost in these woods, Mia.'

'It was an easy mistake,' I told her. 'I was far too busy enjoying the scenery, and I must have missed a couple of flags.'

'Hmm, I doubt that very much.'

'Miss Ross, we don't *know* that Mia didn't get lost of her own accord.' Sebastian strode alongside us, his jaw taut.

'Sebastian, you know as well as I do that young Felicity had a hand in this. In all the years we've been doing these exercises, *nobody* has missed a flag. Felicity is behind this because she is unruly and petulant and...'

'Bitchy.' I waded in with my opinion and Miss Ross cackled. 'Indeed.'

Sebastian paused on the top step and rubbed his hands over his face. He looked tired.

'She is still a student and I have an obligation to protect her as much as anyone else in this academy.'

'With all due respect, Sebastian, you do everything you can for these students, but your talents lie in the management and structure of their education rather than their emotional welfare.'

Well, that explained his lack of paternal instincts. I'd wondered if his coolness towards me had been down to the distant relationship with my dad but now I understood. He didn't know anything about teenagers, especially teenage girls.

'Mia, could you wait in my office, please.'

I nodded at him and thanked Miss Ross for her kindness. Pushing open the front door, I wandered through the foyer to Sebastian's office. The store room door was closed and I couldn't resist trying the handle as I went by. Locked. How did Felicity have a key? I made a mental note to ask Elizabeth if her friend Adam had a set of keys to the academy's many rooms.

The lights were blazing in Sebastian's office and there was a fire roaring in the grate. I warmed my hands before ambling over to his desk. Documents and open books littered the surface. He had obviously been in the middle of something when I strayed out of the treeline. I glanced at the papers filled with data that made no sense to me.

I was about to flop into the chair opposite the desk when a Manila file caught my eye. The label in the top-right corner read 'Private & Confidential—Fatalities'. Taking a quick peek through the window, I saw Sebastian and Miss Ross were still deep in conversation, so I risked a look at the file.

There were lists of names inside the folder, dating back to the 1970s. Three column headings stood out on the crumpled page. Name, Drug Trial Administered, Date of Death. I ran my finger along the long list of names until I reached the bottom of the page. My heart froze. The last name was Cassandra Roberts. My hands began to tremble as I read the information alongside her name. Trial notes: Prototype 0118 failed. Subject fell into a coma. Bite site infection. Unable to resuscitate. Date of Death: October 11th.

My chest was tight as I fought against the tidal wave of tears that threatened to fall, and I found it difficult to breathe. The back of my throat burned, but I refused to allow myself to cry. Sebastian would be here any minute and I was reading his private files. *His* files. Files that contained information about my mother's death.

Memories of my brother's arms wrapped tightly around me barrelled to the front of my mind. He held me as I wept, both of us listening to the police officer who told our father about the hit-and-run driver who had left our mother by the roadside. Zak's strength had kept me glued together over the weeks that followed.

He was fifteen and I had just turned six. Our dad had lost it, drinking more than usual in a miserable attempt to blot out his pain. The shouting was too much for me, and I would sit on my bed with my hands clasped over my ears, blocking out the sounds of Zak and Dad screaming at one another. Zak left me a year later. Mum's death hit our family hard. A tragic accident that tore us apart. And it was all a lie.

SIX

By some miracle, Sebastian was called away to deal with a parent and Miss Ross excused me for the rest of the day.

'The other girls should be at the halfway marker by now and won't start returning until dinner,' she said. 'Go get a shower and enjoy your free time.'

I avoided eye contact as she happily chatted about having the school to myself. If I raised my head, she'd know I was upset. It was torture keeping my emotions in check as she prattled on. A loud crash in the cafeteria attracted her attention and I used the distraction to shoot off up the staircase.

The corridors were deserted as I'd expected, and the silence hit me with such force that when I finally reached the bathroom, I slid to the floor and sobbed. I was still crying when I stepped under the hot stream of water and washed away the dirt and sweat from my unsuccessful run.

Why had the police lied to us about Mum's death? The strange file on Sebastian's desk referred to an infected bite. A sense of clarity settled over me as I realised what that meant. A werewolf killed my dad, his throat ripped out in front of me, and now it seemed that my mum had also died because of a werewolf bite. Becoming a hunter suddenly made absolute sense.

Sebastian was somehow involved, but I couldn't figure out if he was covering for someone or being protective. The photographs of my family in his office could be a sign of guilt or love. Whatever it was, I intended to find out. I made a vow to myself that as soon as Elizabeth returned from the marathon, I would confide in her. My stomach churned as I thought about opening up to someone new, but I wanted to tell her everything. For nine years I'd dealt with life alone, and now I knew it didn't have to be that way. Zak was the only person I'd ever spoken to about things that mattered. He was my best friend and brother rolled into one. Until he left. Then I didn't have anyone to share my pathetic dreams and stories with.

'Be careful who you trust.' Twice in as many days those words had been spoken to me, first by Terry, at the motorway services and earlier this morning by Cody. Although I couldn't trust my uncle or Miss Ross, I could turn to my friend. I needed her help. Someone had to know about the academy. Cody said he had heard bad things about this place. Maybe his brothers knew more.

Determination powered my actions as I threw on my jeans and jumper, pulled on my tattered old Converse and dragged my wet hair back into a ponytail. Cody had mentioned that even though he lived deep in the woods, he often visited the town, and Miss Ross did tell me to enjoy my free time. She didn't specify I had to stay on school property.

•• • ● • ••

MY DARING ESCAPE plan was going smoothly until I bumped into Adam as I skulked around the side of the building heading for the animal cages and the tracks beyond. Feeling flustered, I made up some lame story about exploration.

'You want to explore the forest?' he asked with some trepidation in his voice when I voiced my hastily hatched lie.

'Well, it's such a beautiful day and I love being in nature.' We both looked up at the overcast sky and the grey storm clouds rolling in as the words passed my lips.

'Uh huh.' He wasn't convinced.

Shit.

'Okay, truth is I need to escape this place for a few hours. I'm going stir crazy and Elizabeth won't be back for ages.'

His eyes twinkled at the mention of Elizabeth's name and I couldn't help but smile.

'You want me to keep you company?' he asked.

'Thanks, but I think I need some time alone.' I was genuinely touched that Adam was willing to give up his time for me, but I was on a mission, and nothing would deter me.

'Fair enough,' he said. 'If you stick to the left-hand track it leads down into town where you'll find a few stores and Taylor's Coffee Shop. Don't be long because Lizzie will kill me if anything happens to you.'

The track did indeed lead into town, or at least to a farmer's gate at the top of the high street, which I climbed over, then I headed down the hill.

I'm not sure I would call Ravenshood a town. With only a smattering of local shops, one pub, a church and a bandstand, it looked more like those photographs of rural villages from the geography textbooks we'd had at my last school.

I spotted Taylor's Coffee Shop in the distance with its brightly painted green window frames and potted bay trees either side of the main entrance. The chalkboard outside boasted the best Bakewell pudding in Nottinghamshire. I dug into my jeans pocket and pulled out the ten pound note Sebastian had given me for emergencies. A cake sounded like the perfect fuel to inspire my search for Cody.

A plump lady in a Robin Hood apron smiled at me as I approached the counter.

'Hello, my love, what can I get for you?'

'Hot chocolate and a slice of Bakewell pudding, please.'

She busied herself with my order as I thought about my next tactic. If Ravenshood was indeed a small community, the smiling woman adding a mountain of whipped cream to my mug might know where I could find a certain farm boy.

'Do you know if Cody lives nearby?' I tried to act nonchalant, but the burning sensation rising up my neck and spreading to my cheeks was a bit of a giveaway.

The lady lifted her eyes to meet mine and studied me for a long moment.

'Friend of the Mills family, are you?'

'Er, yes, Cody and I are friends but I've mislaid his address. I'm from out of town and promised I'd pop in for a visit the next time I was here.' I was babbling but couldn't seem to stop. If she believed anything that poured out of my mouth, it would be a miracle.

She finished with the cream and shook a small silver canister over the mug, showering everything in chocolate flakes.

'Cody will be in soon for his lunch. He delivers produce to Mr Thompson over the road and always stops for a cheese roll before heading home.'

I handed over my money and tried to resist the urge to do a little jig on the spot. My face felt warm again and I had an odd sensation in the pit of my stomach.

I positioned myself strategically at a table for two on the left of the entrance.

The café owner was right and just as the hands on the clock above the counter turned to one o'clock I saw a truck pull up opposite the café. The signage down the side panel confirmed that it belonged to the Mills Family Farm. Cody climbed out of the passenger side and lifted a box of vegetables from the back of the truck. He wore the same jeans from earlier but a new T-shirt beneath a navy apron. The muscles on his arms flexed as he hoisted the box up onto his shoulder and disappeared into Mr Thompson's store.

I wiped my hands down my jeans and cursed the butter-flies that were swirling around my stomach. I remembered thinking how good-looking he was when we first met in the forest, but as I sat staring through the window, I realised I'd underestimated how much. Cody was gorgeous. Drop-dead, blonde hair, blue eyes gorgeous. The stuff of movies or rock bands. I dragged the band out of my hair and shook out my ponytail, letting my long hair fall around my shoulders. I heard a chuckle from behind the counter but refused to turn around. I knew I was having a girlie moment, but I didn't need to see the café owner's amused expression.

The door to the coffee shop swung open and a large man with a square jaw and shaggy brown hair stepped inside.

'Afternoon, Jane.' His voice boomed across the café and made me jump.

'Hello, Byron, usual is it?'

'That'll be great, thanks love. I'm starving. Do me a cheese roll for Cody while you're at it.'

I wanted to turn around and look at the man now stand-ing at the counter. This had to be one of Cody's brothers, some-one who could give me answers, but I kept my eyes fixed on Mr Thompson's shop. Cody hadn't come out yet and I didn't want to miss his entrance.

There was a hushed conversation behind me, and I real-ised too late that Jane was making Byron aware of my exis-tence. I stayed as still as possible, straining to hear what she was whispering.

I nearly flew out of my chair when a large hand landed on my right shoulder.

'Hello miss, I understand you're a friend of my little brother.'

Byron slid into the seat opposite me and smiled. His eyes were warm and filled with good humour. He was clearly enjoy-ing seeing me squirm.

'How does a pretty young lass like you know our Cody?'

'We, I...'

Shit.

He smiled again, wider this time until I could see nearly all of his perfectly white teeth.

'No need to be shy. We could be family if the two of you are, you know, a couple.' He winked and his shoulders began to shake as he laughed.

'Oh, no, we're not a couple.' I said, finally finding my voice. 'We haven't known each other very long. I'm new in town and he's the only person I know. Sort of.'

Byron rested his elbows on the table and scrutinised me.

'That's a shame. I think you'd make a lovely girlfriend for my baby brother.'

I felt my cheeks grow hotter as I lowered my gaze and nibbled on my lower lip. How had I got myself into this?

Byron roared with laughter and slapped a big hand on the tabletop.

'I'm sorry. I'm only teasing. It's not often we get pretty strangers in Ravenshood. I don't mean anything by it.'

I looked up at him and found it easy to return his warm smile. His eyes twinkled with mischief, and I remembered when Zak used to look at me in the same way when he was teasing me about something or other. I suddenly missed my brother more than ever.

The café door opened and Cody breezed in with a big smile and a cheery hello for Jane. His eyes slid towards Byron and me and he stopped dead, still clutching the door handle.

'What are you doing here?'

He looked shocked and confused, but he also looked scared. His eyes flicked between Byron and me as if he'd caught us doing something wrong.

Byron didn't seem to notice his brother's discomfort and stood up, swinging his arm across the newly vacated chair.

'I was just keeping your seat warm, baby brother.'

Cody finally released the door and took a tentative step towards me. I tried to keep my face as neutral as possible. I was just a girl in a coffee shop enjoying a hot chocolate and hoping to make a friend.

I smiled up at him in the hope that he would take that as a peace offering. It appeared to work as he slowly lowered himself into the seat. His long fingers rapped at the tabletop and his left leg bounced up and down on the spot. He had either become really shy since our time spent in the woods or he was a nanosecond away from making an escape.

'I'm sorry. I didn't mean to surprise you,' I said finally, keeping my voice low so Byron and Jane couldn't hear.

He looked at me then, his intense blue eyes boring a hole into my soul.

'What you said to me earlier about the academy, I need to ask you about that. I didn't know how else to find you.'

He nodded and wiped his hands down his apron, constantly glancing behind me at where his brother was talking to Jane.

'We can't talk here. It's not safe. Meet me in the woods after dark.'

It seemed odd to assume the woods were safe after dark, and if I arranged to meet him, I was agreeing to something I knew was against Sebastian's rules. However, if Cody had answers, then it was worth the risk.

'Where shall I meet you?'

'There are some cages on the edge of the academy's land. If you follow the track on the right, you'll eventually come to the overhang where we first met. I'll meet you there at midnight.'

He took a pen from his apron pocket and scribbled something on a napkin, then slid it across the table towards me.

'Here's my number just in case you have any problems.'

Without waiting for an answer, he got up and walked over to his brother. Muttering his thanks to Jane, he took a foil-wrapped sandwich from her.

Cody stormed out of the coffee shop but Byron stopped by my table.

'It was lovely to meet you...' He spread out his hands and widened his eyes as he waited for me to fill in the blank.

'Mia.' I said. 'Nice to meet you too.'

Byron took a step backwards as if I'd slapped him. He looked through the window to where Cody was climbing into the truck and then back at me.

'Right, of course, Mia.' His smile was growing thinner by the second, and with a tight nod of his head he rushed for the exit. I watched him fumble with the door handle, all the earlier bravado and jokes a distant memory.

I'd never seen anyone screech the tyres on a truck before, but the Mills Family Farm vehicle left a cough-inducing cloud of dust as Byron tore off down the high street.

Perhaps Cody had told his brother about our earlier meeting and that I was a student at the notorious Hood Academy. There was so much I wanted to know. So much I needed to know.

I looked up at the clock above the counter. Only another ten hours until I saw Cody again. Maybe then I'd get some answers.

·· • ● • ··

WHEN ELIZABETH BURST through our bedroom door looking like a cross between the swamp monster and a yeti, I couldn't resist laughing at my roommate's misfortune.

'It's not funny!' Elizabeth squelched across the floor towards the bathroom, shedding clothing as she went.

'I know, I'm sorry. How was the marathon?'

'Oh, you know. Long, tiring, wet and bloody awful.'

'I'll see if I can rustle us up a couple of hot chocolates from the canteen.'

I left her to shower in peace and made my way downstairs. Clusters of students huddled in the corridors and sat on the stairs wrapped in blankets and dressing gowns, sipping from steaming mugs of chocolatey goodness.

I spotted Felicity and her squad languishing on the sofas in the entrance hall. She glanced at me as I walked towards the canteen, a look of surprise and then malice registering on her features. She was evidently hoping I was still lost in the woods.

Now wasn't the time to confront her. I was happy to wait until the right moment to take my revenge on that bitch. In the meantime, I was going to follow Sebastian's orders and keep out of her way.

•• • ● • ••

ARMED WITH TWO mugs and a large packet of popcorn, I hurried back to our room. Elizabeth should be out of the shower by now. She was easy to talk to, and although I didn't want her to get mixed up in my crazy life, I knew the time had come to ask for help. It was new territory for me and my palms were slick just thinking about it.

Surrounded by an army of stuffed animals, Elizabeth flicked through a schoolbook as I walked in.

'I'm sure they'll let you off doing your homework for one day,' I said, handing her one of the mugs.

Sitting opposite her, I watched as she sipped her hot chocolate and let out a contented sigh. Her long blonde hair was wet and hung loosely around her shoulders, and her bright eyes sparkled in the lamplight. I could see why Adam was so enamoured with her. Elizabeth was one of those rare people who were beautiful on the inside as well as the outside.

'Miss Ross told me you got back first. She mentioned something about you getting lost again.'

I nodded and fished a marshmallow out of my drink before answering. 'Yeah, I missed a couple of flags and ended up in the middle of nowhere.'

'Hmm, I agree with Miss Ross about your missing flags. It had to be Felicity.'

I waved my hand dismissively. 'I don't care about Felicity's stupid prank. As it happens I met a boy who helped me find my way back.'

That got her attention. She put the mug down on the dressing table and shuffled forward until she was teetering on the edge of her bed.

'A boy? Who is he? Is he cute? Ooh, tell me all about him.'

I laughed at her wide-eyed expression. 'Are you obsessed with boys and romance or something?'

'No, but I believe there is a soulmate for each of us, and if we find someone who makes us happy, we should cherish every moment.'

'Is that how you feel about Adam?'

Elizabeth's face lit up at the mention of Hood Academy's groundsman. 'Adam is sweet, kind and warm-hearted, and I love spending time with him.'

'Is he a good kisser?'

I watched her cheeks grow pink as she squirmed on the bed. 'We've only kissed a couple of times and only recently.'

'What took you so long?'

Elizabeth frowned. 'We had to overcome certain...problems.'

Now I was intrigued.

'Adam only arrived at the academy a month ago,' she continued. 'I'm sure you can imagine the impression he made on the girls—one girl in particular.'

'Felicity!'

Elizabeth nodded and dunked a marshmallow with the tip of her finger.

'Felicity flirted with him outrageously. It was embarrassing.'

I stifled a laugh at Elizabeth's horrified expression.

'So what happened? Did he only have eyes for you?'

She blushed. 'I used to share a room with Felicity and just before you arrived here she found me and Adam...together.'

I was aware that my mouth was open but no sound came out. The revelation that sweet, gentle Lizzie had been paired up with that red-headed monster startled me more than the love triangle.

'Felicity went mad. She was screaming and shouting, and in the end Adam dragged me out of the room for my own safety. Miss Ross assigned me a new room, this one, and I tried to keep out of Felicity's way.'

'Something we have in common,' I mumbled.

'Felicity tried to get Adam fired while Sebastian was out of town collecting you, but Miss Ross was brilliant and stood up to the governors. I don't think Felicity will ever forgive me.'

'Well, all I can say is Adam has great taste. He's smitten with you, that's obvious.'

'Do you really think so?'

'Hell yeah. When I mentioned your name earlier, his eyes twinkled. Of course, that was when he helped me escape the academy.'

Elizabeth's head jerked up at the mention of my extracurricular activities, and she scrunched her brow.

'Why did you want to escape?'

I took a deep breath and launched into my day's activities, then told her about Cody appearing in the woods and the strange conversation about Hood Academy.

'If I hadn't got lost and met Cody, I may never have ended up in Sebastian's office and seen the file on his desk.'

I paused to check she was taking it all in. She studied me for a moment then urged me to continue with a wave of her hand.

'The file was a list of fatalities and at the bottom was my mum's name. There's more to Hood Academy than just training and taking an oath. I think Cody can help me find out what that is, so I'm meeting him again. Tonight. At midnight.'

'Are you crazy?' She jumped off the bed and began pacing the floor. 'You can't meet a strange boy in the woods and especially not in the middle of the night. It's too dangerous.'

'I know it sounds dangerous, but I'll be careful. It's odd but I feel like I can trust Cody.'

'You don't know anything about him!' Elizabeth placed her hands on her hips and towered over me as I sat on my bed.

'I know you're worried about me, but I can take care of myself, and besides, I need to know what he was talking about. There's something going on at this school that potentially involves my family. Something is not as it should be and I need to find out what it is.'

Her shoulders sagged as all the fight drained out of her.

'I'll come with you,' she said.

I wasn't expecting that. Elizabeth was full of surprises, and it felt nice to be able to confide in someone and have them back me up.

'I can't ask you to do that, but I do need your help. Do you think you could ask Adam for a spare key to the front door?'

She flopped down on her bed and wrapped her arms around herself.

'The front door is bolted from the inside after lights out, but he does have a key to the kitchen door. I'll ask him.'

We smiled at one another and I had the strangest sensation of being at peace. I'd shared a part of my life with someone and they hadn't pushed me away or laughed at me.

'Thanks, Lizzie,' I whispered.

She came and sat next to me, threading her arm in mine and resting her head on my shoulder.

'That's what friends are for.'

Friends. I had a friend. Zak would be so proud.

·· • ● • ··

ADAM AND ELIZABETH turned out to be the best wingmen anyone could wish for. Adam gave me a spare key to the back door off the main kitchen that led to a dark courtyard which housed the wheelie bins. A short jog across the side lawn took me to the animal cages and the track that Cody told me to follow. Adam even loaned me a torch and a black waterproof jacket.

Elizabeth pushed a small penknife into my hand with strict instructions to use it if my life was threatened. I sincerely hoped it wouldn't come to that.

They waved me off and told me they would wait up until I returned. I prayed that I would come back in one piece. Glancing up at the night sky, I noticed the moon had started to wane, and once again I kicked myself for not asking Miss Ross how many nights the wolves would be roaming the forest.

•• • ● • ••

I FOUND THE overhang easily this time as if I'd memorised the route after using it so many times. Ravenshood lay below me, the town in darkness apart from the odd lamp in a window. The air was so still that all I could hear was the beating of my heart.

'You made it. Did you have any trouble finding this place?'

I spun around at the sound of the voice behind me. Cody stood a short distance away dressed in dark jeans and a black jacket. He looked like a secret agent. I tried not to think about his role as the next James Bond and dropped my gaze to his feet.

'No, your instructions were spot on, thank you.'

He gave a short nod of his head.

'So, what do you need to know?' he asked.

His question surprised me. He had been so elusive and cold before that I assumed it would be difficult to get any information out of him tonight. Either I'd misread the signs of his earlier inner struggle at the coffee shop, or he didn't have the answers I wanted.

'You told me that Hood Academy was a bad place. What did you mean?'

He gestured for us to sit on the boulders that looked out over the valley. I dropped down and swung my legs over the ledge as Cody did the same. His thigh brushed up against me, but he didn't flinch away this time. Instead, he remained that way with his leg touching mine. My mouth went dry. I tried to concentrate on anything other than the sensation of how close he was to me. If I could have slapped myself without looking like a total fool, I would have.

I cleared my throat and tried again. 'I know I've only been at the school for a couple of days, but I don't see any evidence that it's a bad place.'

I hoped he wouldn't notice the quiver in my voice as I lied. The screams from the store room certainly pointed towards something very bad happening within the walls, and then there was the list with my mum's name on it, but did he know any more than I did? I didn't want to blurt out everything I'd discovered until I was sure I could trust him to be honest with me.

'It's mostly myth and legend that surrounds Hood Academy, but something bad seems to happen to people who come into contact with the students,' he said. 'According to my brothers, the superstitions surrounding the school have been passed down over many generations. Did you know Queen Victoria is supposed to have opened it?'

I smiled, remembering the small book Sebastian had given me with the reference to Dr Neale, the master werewolf hunter for the realm.

'Yeah, I heard that the original owner worked for royalty.'

'Well, Byron told me the old queen believed in the supernatural, and so she founded the school to protect the town.'

'Supernatural? You mean like vampires and stuff?'

Cody nodded, his blonde hair falling across his face. He swept it back in one fluid motion and continued with his story.

'Yes, but I don't think it was vampires that she was worried about.'

He was clearly gearing up to break the news that werewolves were real, and I felt a bubble of panic rise up my spine. Was I supposed to act shocked when he announced it? Should I scream like a girl and run or should I express disbelief? He saved me from doing anything.

'Of course, it's all a load of rubbish. Theory has it that a big dog bit someone and the townsfolk got all hysterical. The reports were twisted and by the time they reached the queen she believed that huge beasts were roaming the forests. Everyone knows that it's not true.'

He looked out over the valley, and I took the opportunity to study his profile. Any girl would kill for his cheekbones. He had the most handsome face, with a strong jaw, but I couldn't help settling my gaze on the fullness of his lips. I had a brief desire to see if they tasted as good as they looked. He sensed me staring and swung round to look at me. I was thankful for the darkness so he couldn't see me blushing.

'So, according to the town's history, my school was created to scare away big dogs?'

Cody chuckled. 'Told you it was rubbish. The stories have escalated over the years and now the entire town believes the academy, and its students, are cursed.'

I wasn't buying it. When he had helped me out of the tree, he was visibly shaken when I'd mentioned Hood Academy, and earlier at the coffee shop he hadn't been pleased to see me. He didn't seem the sort of guy who believed in curses. So why was he feeding me a useless story? Unless he did know the truth but couldn't tell me and was fobbing me off. It was time to call his bluff.

'Well, that's a shame,' I said. 'I was hoping you would be able to tell me more about the werewolf pack and why my fellow students are training to kill them.'

SEVEN

The silence stretched out between us as I watched every kind of emotion flash across his pale face. Eventually, he settled on a deep sigh and a defeated slump of his shoulders.

'I think you need to start from the beginning,' I said, folding my arms like a disgruntled teacher. 'There's no curse. The school is a training centre for wannabe werewolf hunters, and we both know it.'

In the fading light of the moon, I noticed the anguish in Cody's expression. The breath caught in my throat and I grabbed his hand, squeezing his fingers.

'I'm sorry, Cody. I never meant to be so blunt about it.'

Damn! Maybe he *did* believe in the curse story, after all.

He rubbed at his face with his free hand but kept the fingers of his other hand wrapped tightly around mine. I felt a warmth spread down my limbs.

'It's okay,' he whispered. 'I guess I'm actually relieved that you know.'

My quizzical expression urged him on.

'All my life my dad told me to keep the town's wolf secrets to myself. Byron said it's all hush-hush for a reason and if we start talking about the werewolves, then it'll attract bad luck. When you told me you'd just arrived at the academy, I was worried that you either didn't know about the place, or you were going to go all ninja on me.'

'You think the hunters are a danger to the town?'

'Yes, I've seen some of the students in action, and when they get started it doesn't end well.'

'You've seen them kill a werewolf?'

'No, I've seen them attack a boy because they *suspected* he was a werewolf. I wasn't sure if you were the same as them.'

I squeezed his fingers. 'I'm not.'

He smiled down at me and held my gaze. It was like he could read my thoughts, see into my soul. I suddenly felt exposed—naked. I averted my eyes and looked out over the sleeping town.

'Do you and your family know where the wolves are?' I asked, filling the silence.

'They keep to themselves and if people don't bother them, they don't stray near to town. The folk here keep the peace with the wolves but that's at risk if your school keeps churning out Barbie-sized hunters.'

I burst out laughing at his comment and made him jump.

'I'm sorry, but now you mention it, it's kind of true. There's a particular student who fits the plastic doll stereotype perfectly.'

Looking down at my hand, I examined our entwined fingers. Cody wasn't in any rush to let go, so I relished the feel of his rough hand in mine and the warmth that continued to vibrate through our connection.

'So, that's why you said Hood Academy is a bad place, because it threatens the truce between Ravenshood and the wolves.'

He dropped his gaze to study our interwoven hands, rotating them so that his was on top of mine. It felt strangely comforting.

'There's a rumour in town that the students at Hood Academy capture the wolves and do experiments on them in class.'

I flinched involuntarily. Sebastian hadn't mentioned any kind of warped biology lesson to me, but that didn't mean that Cody wasn't right. I'd only been at the school a few days and didn't know enough about the curriculum to confirm or deny Cody's rumour.

A memory of the late-night screams rumbled through my mind. Was it true? Did the student body catch the wolves and keep them locked up until it was time for a macabre show-and-tell?

I quickly steered the conversation around to basic werewolf legend, eager to find out more about this mythological species. 'Is it true that the werewolves only stay in their wolf form on the night of a full moon?'

Cody lifted his head and looked over at me, his bright blue eyes filling my vision.

'They always turn on a full moon but can also change at will in case they need to defend themselves...according to Byron.'

'So if your rumour was true, the school would be full of extra people and not animals.'

'I guess so, unless they stayed in their animal form as a method of defence.'

The very human-sounding scream that had come from the underground lab told me the captive wasn't in wolf form.

'What if they couldn't remain in their wolf mode?' I whispered.

Cody's eyes shone in the soft moonlight as his gaze trailed over my face. He lingered a moment on my lips.

'If they couldn't stay in wolf form, I dread to think what your classmates might do to them.'

'You sound like it's a bad thing that the school experiments on them. Not that I'm condoning animal testing or anything, but surely if the students kill the werewolves, your town is safe.'

'It's not that simple, Mia. Ninety-nine per cent of the time they are as human as you or me, and they don't deserve to be harmed. Not for any reason. Whether there are good intentions at the bottom of it or not.'

I looked out over the valley as I digested Cody's words. He was right of course. No creature deserved to be in pain, and the screams I'd heard the other night proved that someone was indeed getting hurt. Could I trust Cody with what I knew? I'd trusted Elizabeth and Adam and they hadn't let me down so far. Perhaps my luck would continue.

'I can find out if the rumours are true,' I said softly, studying his face for any spark of mistrust.

'You'd put yourself in danger for the werewolves? Aren't you going to be training to hunt them down?'

'Yes, on both counts. At the moment, I've had light lessons but my full training starts tomorrow. I'm going to learn what they have to teach me, Cody, but I have no intention of using those skills to harm anyone...or anything.'

He smiled at me and this time it reached his eyes. The tight smile from yesterday had vanished and he appeared calmer and more relaxed. I was still very conscious of our hands tightly clasped and our legs touching. My stomach did a strange lurch as my neck and cheeks flamed. I was grateful for the cool early morning air.

We sat in comfortable silence for a long time, watching the slumbering town and listening to the nocturnal activity surrounding us. I felt peaceful and dare I say it, safe. I never wanted to leave the calming influence of the forest. Being in Cody's company was enjoyable as he felt like a kindred spirit, but I knew Elizabeth and Adam would worry if I didn't return soon.

'I better get back before anyone misses me.'

Cody got to his feet and pulled me up so I was standing beside him. His scent was intoxicating, and I vowed to remember that smell so I could recall it whenever I wanted to reminisce about this night—this moment.

'Promise me you'll be careful, Mia.' He ran his thumb down my cheek, and I swear I felt an explosion go off in my head. 'Your uncle won't want you snooping around, so be on your guard.'

I couldn't answer as he leant in and pressed his lips to mine, softly at first but then applying light pressure.

His hands cupped my face as he pulled away and smiled down at me.

'I don't want anything bad to happen to you, Mia. For the first time since my parents' death, I feel like I've found someone I can talk to properly. Someone who understands me.'

A glow spread through me at his touch and his words. I knew exactly what he meant. I'm not sure that Zak would have approved of me snogging in the middle of the woods at midnight, but I believed that he would have liked Cody and that filled my heart with hope. An emotion I thought I'd never experience again.

'You've got my number. Message me when you know more and we'll meet back here,' he said, brushing my hair behind my ear.

I nodded and leant into his hand, kissing his palm as it swept down my face.

'Okay,' I said. 'I'll find out as much as I can.'

He kissed me again, full on the lips, taking my breath away, before turning and disappearing into the treeline. I stood for a while in silence, willing my heart to stop thumping so loud. It wasn't my first kiss, that prize had gone to Tom Nook in the last year of junior school, but this was like nothing I'd ever experienced. I touched my fingertips to my lips and smiled. Life had taken a turn for the better.

Adam was still awake when I tiptoed into the bedroom. He was leaning against the wall with Elizabeth's head resting on his chest. She was out cold and oblivious to my stealthy return. Adam smiled as I closed the door behind me.

'You're alive,' he whispered with a wide grin.

I snorted as I untied my shoes and kicked them into the corner.

'So how did it go?'

'It went better than I thought. Cody was...very helpful.'

Adam bent his head to the side and watched me carefully. I felt every inch the naughty schoolgirl.

'That good, eh?' He winked and I felt my face grow hot.

I ignored his knowing smirk.

'Cody told me about the werewolves and a pact between them and the town. From the sound of it, Hood Academy is the threat, not the wolves. The townsfolk believe that we're experimenting on the werewolves as part of our science classes.'

Adam's eyes widened and I had a moment of panic when I thought he was going to say that Werewolf Dissection 101 was at nine o'clock the next morning.

'That explains the noises,' he mumbled.

'What noises? Do you know something?'

'When I started working here, I was given a bunch of master keys. I can access every classroom, office and door in this place. The other day, I unlocked the store room in the foyer.'

'You went inside?'

He nodded. 'Yes, but just for a second. I heard this faint grumbling and moaning sound coming from behind the shelves. Your uncle arrived and ushered me out, so I couldn't investigate.'

'What did he say?'

'He told me I was imagining the sounds and said it was only a stationery store. Then he took my key off me.'

'I saw Felicity go inside the other night,' I confessed. 'She took one of her heavies in with her and I managed to follow for a bit. The store room opens up to a long corridor with stairs leading down to a basement room.'

I paused as I let Adam digest everything I was saying. He knew this school better than I did, and I was pretty sure he trusted his employer. Was I about to shatter all his misconceptions? Would this knowledge put his career at risk?

'I didn't see what they were doing down there,' I continued, 'but I heard someone screaming. It sounded like a man or a boy; definitely human.'

We sat in silence for a moment listening to the soft snores from Elizabeth, neither one of us wanting to admit that whatever we thought we knew was not as bad as the reality could be.

'I can try and get my hands on that key again,' he said, stroking his hand down Elizabeth's golden hair. 'The three of us will work out what's going on.'

'The three of us?'

'Yes. Elizabeth and I were talking about it while you were gone and we want to help. You can't do this on your own, Mia. You need extra eyes and ears and we can provide that. Your uncle will be checking on you and that puts you in full view of the one person we're trying to avoid.'

'So, if he's watching me, he won't be watching you.'

'Exactly!'

I flopped back on my bed and stared at the ceiling. In such a short time I'd gone from a beaten and broken girl to werewolf hunter and spy. I wondered what Zak would think if he knew.

Adam slid out from under Elizabeth and lowered her head to the pillow. He bent over and kissed her tenderly on the cheek. I smiled to myself, recalling my first kiss with Cody earlier this evening. I was still reeling from it and if I hadn't been so exhausted, I might have sat up all night reliving it.

'Take care of yourself, Mia.' Adam said, climbing up on the desk and throwing his leg out of the window to descend the waiting ladder.

'I will. Promise me you'll be careful too.' I didn't want him risking anything for me.

He nodded and then disappeared from view, his dark skin blending in with the darkness.

Elizabeth stirred and opened her eyes.

'You're alive,' she said, her voice croaky from sleep.

I chuckled as she mimicked Adam's exact reaction on seeing me again.

'I'm alive. It went well. Cody was helpful but I think I can find out more here at the school. Do you remember the file I mentioned, the one with my mum's name on it?'

Elizabeth nodded.

'Well, it also had a number; prototype 0118. I need to find out what experiments they did on her and why.'

Elizabeth yawned and I noticed how late it was.

'Go back to sleep and we'll talk more in the morning.'

Her lips twitched in a half-asleep smile and she was steadily snoring again before I could turn off the light.

Starting tomorrow I was going to embrace everything Hood Academy could teach me. I was going to take that hunter oath, and then I was going to use it all to discover the truth about my mum's death, the werewolves and the part my mysterious uncle had to play in it all.

EIGHT

reakfast at Hood Academy was a messy affair. I sat next to Elizabeth at the far side of the room, keeping a wary eye out for Felicity. I still owed her for getting me lost in the woods, but, without her assistance, however ill-intentioned, I might never have met Cody. Maybe I should be thanking her instead of thumping her.

Miss Ross appeared in the doorway and waved me over.

'I guess my training is about to begin,' I murmured to Elizabeth as I cleared my plate and dropped it in the used crock bucket.

'Good luck!' Elizabeth's sing-song voice followed me as I weaved in and out of the breakfast tables.

Sebastian had decided to pull me from certain classes so I could have one-on-one sessions with Miss Ross. He wanted me to catch up so I could integrate fully into class activities as soon as possible. I should have been glad that I was getting out of double maths, but looking at the glint in Miss Ross's eye I doubted I was getting off lightly.

We walked across the grounds and back to the gym that she had shown me on my original tour. I spotted Adam cutting the grass as we marched down the gravel path. His head lifted as we trotted past and he raised a hand in greeting.

'Such a nice lad,' Miss Ross said as she waved back.

'Yes, he is.'

•• • ● • ••

THE GYM WAS just as I remembered it, and I couldn't shake the feeling of being at an army training camp. Two large blue mats filled the centre of the room and there was a long staff at each corner. They were the same weapons I'd seen the girls using on the front lawn the day I arrived. About five foot long and smooth to the touch. There were two black rubber strips equally spaced along the staff for ease of handling. The way my palms were sweating, I could imagine causing additional damage to the surrounding area if that thing slipped from my grasp.

'Grip the staff like so.' Miss Ross flicked the weapon off the floor. She stood in the centre of one blue mat with her feet together.

I lifted the other staff from the floor and mirrored her stance on the opposite mat.

'When you start to fight, bring your less dominant leg and arm to the front. This allows you to swing your dominant arm forward with more strength, like so.'

She lurched forward, bouncing on the balls of her feet and flipping the wooden staff forward at a tremendous pace. If I had been standing a foot closer, my nose would have been a bloody mess right now.

'In a few weeks Hood Academy holds its annual sparring assessment. If we get your training up to an agreeable standard, there's no reason why you can't take part.'

'Do I have to?'

'You'll be fine. Besides, the assessment is the perfect stage for taking your hunter oath.'

'You mean the bit where I swear my loyalty to crown and country?'

Miss Ross smiled. 'It's a huge honour, Mia. You get to stand in front of your peers and promise to be a part of something special. A new family if you like.'

I'd had about as much 'family' time as I could stomach, so I shut my mouth and followed Miss Ross's lead.

For the next hour, she taught me how to roundhouse kick, thrust, block and sweep. My arms ached and I was convinced that every inch of my body would be covered in bruises. I needed to work on my defence if I was going to stand any chance against my fellow students.

'You learn fast, Mia. Your uncle will be proud of you.'

It felt strange to hear that. Only Zak had ever used the word proud around me and that was on the day he left. *'You're the best little sister anyone could wish for,'* he had said, *'and I'm so proud to be your brother. Never forget that.'*

'I promised Sebastian that I'd try to fit in here, and if that means I need to throw myself into my training, that's what I'll do.'

'It's not all about school, Mia. Sebastian wants you to be able to defend yourself. I'm sure you wish you'd had this kind of training from an earlier age.'

She glanced over at me with a knowing look on her face and wide, expressive eyes.

'Did Sebastian tell you about my dad?'

'If you mean about the beatings then yes, he did. I'm sorry, Mia. No child should have to put up with that behaviour, especially not from a loving parent.'

I gave a sharp laugh and whirled the staff around in my hands.

'Just for the record, my dad was *not* a loving parent. He was cold, calculating and a violent drunk. If Sebastian knew about that, why didn't he come and get me earlier? Why wait until I had to watch my dad get his throat ripped out by a bloody werewolf?'

Miss Ross watched me carefully as if deciding on the appropriate words.

'Your uncle couldn't interfere even though he wanted to. When your mother died it created a rift between him and your father, and I don't think Sebastian knew how to repair the damage.'

'He didn't have to repair anything, he just had to take me away.' I could feel my shoulders slump as I caved in on myself. It was an automatic reaction whenever I thought about my dad. Like an inbuilt safety mechanism that helped me to shrink away and become invisible.

'Sebastian didn't realise it was that bad, Mia. Give him a chance to make it up to you at least. He cares about you and he can keep you safe.'

'Like he kept my mum safe?'

The dark shadow that flashed across Miss Ross's face told me she knew more than she was telling me. Should I divulge the information I'd found on the file in Sebastian's office? Maybe she could tell me why my mother's death was covered up.

As if sensing my imminent questions, Miss Ross dropped her staff in the storage bucket and headed towards the door. She pulled at the handle and exposed the lush gardens beyond the gym, calling over her shoulder as she went. 'That's all for today, Mia. I'm happy for you to join the rest of the class for group training.'

As she marched off, leaving me alone in the gymnasium, I felt that familiar prickling sensation down my neck. Turning to the bank of windows, I surveyed the forest beyond. Nothing.

I huffed at my reaction. Clearly, Miss Ross's input had unnerved me more than I realised.

• • ● • •

ELIZABETH FOUND ME sulking in the common room a couple of hours later. I'd taken it upon myself to start reading through the textbooks Sebastian had dropped off early this morning. History and science hardbacks together with a volume on myth and legend. Not the kind of schoolbooks I would have had in my old life.

'I'm impressed,' she said. 'I never had you down as the studious type.'

Her eyes twinkled as she teased me and I smiled. It was easy being around Elizabeth. She made me forget that I was ever alone.

'For the record, I've spent my day catching up on schoolwork and learning to fling that bloody staff around. I'm exhausted.'

'Well don't nod off just yet. I've come to collect you for class. You need to survive one more staff-whirling session then you can finish for the day.'

I groaned and Elizabeth laughed. 'You'll be fine, just hide at the back.'

We made our way to the gymnasium with the rest of the student body and took up our positions on the wooden floor. No mats this time. Miss Ross had obviously been extra kind to me earlier.

My stomach lurched as I spotted Felicity stride to the front of the room. If she was running this group, I was in trouble. Elizabeth glanced over at me and gave a little thumbs up sign. She had obviously had the same thought.

'We're going to break off into pairs.' Felicity's voice cut through the air like nails on a chalkboard. 'Try to pick a partner that you've never sparred with.'

There was a rush of movement as the girls scuttled back and forth finding partners. I stepped up to Elizabeth's side and claimed her before anyone else could.

'This will be fun,' she whispered.

I doubted that my mediocre skills with a staff would be any competition for Elizabeth's training.

'You mean fun for you when you whip my ass.'

She giggled. 'Exactly.'

With everyone in position, Felicity blew her whistle and the sound of wood on wood exploded throughout the room. Elizabeth thrust forward with her dominant arm, and I lifted my staff in time to block her advance. I spotted what looked like a mixture of surprise and pride flutter across her face.

We tested one another's skills, breaking through the defensive barriers every now and then, but I was satisfied at being able to hold my own against a more experienced fighter.

As we were so caught up in our training, neither of us saw Felicity approach until she'd lunged forward with her staff, knocking both of us off balance.

'There's no need to go easy on this one,' she said, tossing an icy glare in my direction. 'If anything, we need to push her more than anyone else so she doesn't hold the class back.'

Elizabeth tried to intervene, but I stopped her with a raised hand.

'It's fine, Lizzie. If Felicity thinks I need additional help, who are we to argue? Maybe she could teach me.'

A hush fell over the gymnasium as I took my position across from my nemesis. I knew I didn't stand a chance against her, but if I could get at least one or two brutal swings in I'd be happy.

We circled each other like vultures around a fresh kill. I could feel everyone's eyes on us and prayed that I could land one half-decent strike.

Felicity lurched forward, flipping her staff skyward with her toe. Distracted momentarily by the flying weapon, I didn't see her fist coming. She punched me hard in the stomach and I folded, dropping to my knees.

Over my shoulder, I could hear Elizabeth urging the rest of the group to keep working and hustling them back into pairs. At least if they were occupied, I wouldn't have an audience for my downfall.

Still slightly winded, I slowly dragged myself up to my full height. Felicity was bouncing on her toes, balancing her staff in one hand and grinning at me like a feral cat. If she thought she was leaving this gymnasium without at least one bruise, then she was mistaken.

I whipped my staff up so fast she failed to see it until it connected with her chin. The loud yelp she made when my weapon found its target filled me with hope.

She snarled at me. 'You're going to pay for that.'

I didn't doubt it, but I allowed myself a small moment of pride.

She pushed forward and I blocked her advance. She tried again but I was there to prevent the strike. This carried on for a while, and her frustration was evident in her angry cries. Relentlessly she attacked and I continued to defend myself. Her eyes blazed with pure hatred.

An eerie hush fell over the room as the other students watched our exchange. One of the girls called time, telling us that the class had finished and it was time to leave but nobody dared move.

During the short distraction, Felicity advanced once more and the staff flew out of my grasp as she flipped her own weapon with ease. She swept her leg out, cutting me down at the knee until I was sprawled on the floor, my staff clattering beside me.

I lifted my chin and steadied myself to stand but the butt of Felicity's staff struck me on the side of the head. Stumbling backwards, I landed on my backside.

'Hey, that's not allowed.' Elizabeth's voice splintered the silence.

I waited for the spinning sensation to pass. The last thing I wanted was to throw up in the middle of the gymnasium with everyone watching.

Elizabeth barrelled her way to my side, pushing the girls out of the way until she reached me.

'Leave her alone, Felicity!'

'I'm fine, Lizzie, honestly. It was just a tap.' The spots that swirled across my vision told another story.

Felicity laughed and whirled her staff around her arms like a baton twirler in the middle of a parade.

Grabbing onto Elizabeth's arm for support, I let her pull me up and tug me towards the exit. I didn't want to make a scene. Sebastian had warned me to stay away from Felicity, but I hadn't been able to resist the opportunity to get my own back on her. Maybe it was time I started listening to him. Even if it meant ignoring the smug bitch. As I brushed past her, she hissed in my ear. 'You should be used to getting a smack around the head. Think of it as a cure for homesickness.'

Somewhere on the other side of the hall, I heard someone suck in their breath. The air whooshed out of me as Felicity's words punctured my heart. I felt like I'd floated out of my body and was watching the scene pan out in slow motion below me. The hunter and the hunted.

The clock above the door ticked painfully on to the next second as if the effort to move was too much. Elizabeth's eyes widened and her mouth began to open in readiness to shout something, but I never got to hear what she wanted to say.

From deep within my gut, the rage built up and bubbled over. My fingers tensed and curled into fists as a red fog descended over me, blocking out all sound. The image of my dad's face steamrolled through my mind, and I let out a choked sob. All I could think about was squeezing the life out of the redhead who stood in front of me.

It all happened so fast. My fist connected with Felicity's jaw with such force that we both fell. She crashed to the gymnasium floor with a loud yelp and I landed on top of her, crushing her to the wooden floor.

She squirmed and bucked in an attempt to throw me off, but the anger that roared through my veins held me firmly in place. I straddled her body so that I was sitting on her stomach, my knees pressing into her ribcage, pinning her to the ground as I pounded her face with my fists, repeatedly, left then right.

Her arms flailed as she tried to block my advances, but something had taken over me, a darkness that I'd never felt before.

Then it was no longer Felicity's face that I saw, it was mine, bloody and broken and begging for my father to stop.

With a rush of noise, the world came crashing back down. I could hear the screams and shouts around me and felt Elizabeth's hand pulling at my arm and shouting my name. I looked up into her face and saw the panic in her eyes, then I felt the warmth coating my hands. I flinched as I realised I was still sitting across Felicity, who was screaming hysterically and using her arms to protect herself. The warmth I'd felt was blood, her blood. I'd punched her until her nose bled and her eye began to swell.

'I'm...I'm so sorry.' I jumped up and fled from the gym, Elizabeth right behind me.

OATH BREAKER

NINE

My hands shook as I sat in the armchair facing Sebastian's desk. I hadn't had time to clean myself up before he whisked me into his office. Felicity's blood had dried over my knuckles and I frantically rubbed at it as if this simple act would erase the memory of what I'd just done.

'I warned you to stay away from her.' Sebastian had been shouting at me for the last ten minutes. He hadn't stopped pacing his office and waving his arms in the air.

'She provoked me,' I said again.

Sebastian held his hand out to shut me up, the skin at the corner of his eye twitching as he glared at me in anger. I recoiled involuntarily and his expression softened slightly.

'Felicity's family will demand your expulsion, and I don't know if I can prevent it,' he said, folding his arms across his chest and slumping against the wall.

'I thought *you* ran this school. So much for family loyalty, eh?'

'You really think they care that we are related? That just makes things worse, Mia.'

I shrugged my shoulders. 'Maybe it's not such a bad thing. I could go to school in Ravenshood but still live here, with you.'

He stared at a spot over my right shoulder for what seemed like an eternity then resumed his pacing.

'No, I need you to remain here and continue your training. It's important.'

My ears pricked up at his words and I felt a rumbling of unease.

'Why is it so important to you that I stay here and train to be a hunter? Is it because a werewolf killed my mum?'

He stopped suddenly and spun around to face me, a startled expression on his face.

'What did you say?'

I squared my shoulders and sat up a little straighter in the chair. It was time to test my uncle and his loyalties.

'I saw a list on your desk with my mum's name on it. The cause of death was an infected bite not a hit-and-run. Why didn't you tell me?'

Sebastian sank down into the chair behind his desk and rubbed a hand over his face. He looked exhausted.

'It's true, your mother was killed by a werewolf. You were far too young to understand, and so it was much easier if you thought it was an accident.'

'But you let *all* of us believe it was a car accident. My dad. Zak. We were together when the police came to the door and told us. How could you do that to us?'

I analysed my uncle as he hung his head. Any fear I may have had about standing up for myself vanished and I felt angry. What gave him the right to decide what we knew?

'Were you having an affair with my mum before she died?'

My direct question obviously shocked him as he spluttered an incoherent jumble of words before resting his elbows on the desk and holding his head in his hands.

'I loved your mother very much, but no, we weren't having an affair.'

'Why did you love her? It wasn't your job to love her, it was ours. Me, Zak and Dad. I don't understand how she could be involved with werewolves unless *you* put her in harm's way.'

'Mia, there is so much you don't understand, and that's why it's important that you stay here and train. Werewolves murdered both your parents. Surely that's enough motivation to behave and trust in my judgement.'

I stood up, curling my blood-encrusted fists into tight balls. I'd had enough of people telling me how to behave, and I was fed up of the bullying and all the lies.

'You don't get to decide what's right for me. As you say, werewolves killed my parents and that should be enough motivation to stay the hell away from them.'

Sebastian burst from his chair and was around the desk in a heartbeat. He stood over me and hissed menacingly into my ear. 'I have every right to decide what's right for you, Mia. I'm the only family you have left. Stay here until I work out what to do with you.' With that, he stormed out of his office, slamming the door behind him.

I lowered myself into the chair, afraid that my wobbly legs wouldn't be able to hold me up for much longer. It appeared that my dear uncle Sebastian was more like my dad than I'd first realised. It wasn't long until the tears began to fall. I curled up in a ball and sobbed for a long time.

•• • ● • ••

CONFINED TO SEBASTIAN'S office, I pulled a couple of books from the shelves and busied myself by reading. The rain hammered at the picture window and the fire popped in the grate. For such a big school, full of hundreds of girls, it was extremely quiet.

At three o'clock I heard the rumble of footsteps as the students made their way to the last lesson of the day. Only one hour to wait and then I'd be in for another slanging match with Sebastian. I briefly wondered if he'd starve me to death as part of my punishment. My stomach rumbled as if to confirm my suspicions.

I wandered over to the back wall of Sebastian's office which was made up of floor-to-ceiling bookshelves. There was an impressive library here, intermingled with photo frames of my family. I picked up a picture of my mother taken a few months prior to her death. I remembered her long brown curls and the way her cheek dimpled when she smiled. Sebastian had said he loved her very much but that they weren't having an affair. Did she know he loved her? Is that why she came to the academy so often? Miss Ross had told me she was a frequent visitor.

The door burst open causing me to lose my grip on the frame, which fell to the floor with a crash. Elizabeth stood in the doorway, her brow creased with worry.

I glanced down at the smashed glass of the frame and sighed.

'Jeez, Lizzie, you frightened me to death.'

'Sorry. Dr Roberts let me off my last class so I could come and get you. He's asked me to take you out for something to eat. Even gave me some money.'

I looked across at her, my mouth hanging open.

'Why the hell would he do that? He spent most of the day screaming at me. I'm supposed to be getting expelled, not taken out for a meal.'

'He did mumble something about keeping you well away from the student body until lights out.'

'Ah, so it's a hide her away and deal with it later ploy. How unoriginal.'

I crouched to clear up the glass, dropping it into the bin by the side of Sebastian's desk. The frame wasn't damaged so hopefully he wouldn't notice. As I set it back on the shelf, my mum's photograph slipped out of the bindings and drifted to the floor.

'What's that?' Elizabeth pointed at a yellowing piece of paper hidden behind the photograph with a sealed envelope clipped to the page.

'I don't know.'

As I unfolded the paper, I spotted my mother's handwriting, her expressive curly letters covering the page.

'It's from my mum.' Excitement fluttered in my chest as I started to read.

Elizabeth placed her hand over my arm and tugged me towards the door.

'Maybe you should read it in private. We've been given a free pass and by the look of your puffy eyes, I'd say you need it.'

I smiled at my friend and nodded. Some time away from Hood Academy was just what I needed. Grabbing the broken frame, photograph and letter, I stuffed them inside my training jacket and followed Elizabeth out of the office.

•• ● ••

ADAM WAS WAITING in a beat-up old Ford when we rushed down the front stairs of the school. With the engine running and him glancing backwards and forwards, it made me think of a getaway after a bank robbery. I sniggered to myself as I climbed into the back seat.

'You okay?' Adam glanced at the red welts on my hands.

'Yeah, my fist connected with someone's face.'

'Fair enough.'

Elizabeth jumped into the passenger seat and leant over to give Adam a kiss.

'Thanks for doing this,' she said.

'It's my pleasure. Miss Ross came and found me before you did. She said I might be needed for a speedy escape.'

Elizabeth laughed and slammed the car door behind her.

'Well then, you better do as she asked and get us away from this place.'

'I'm on it.'

The car jolted forward and we made our way down the winding drive. It seemed like an eternity since I had first seen the wrought-iron gates of Hood Academy after my father's death.

•• ● ••

ELIZABETH SUGGESTED GOING to Taylor's Coffee Shop for homemade burgers and chips, and I briefly wondered if Jane, the proprietor, would remember me.

The café was bustling with conversation and laughter when we crowded through the door and settled ourselves into a booth. I sat facing the window, secretly hoping to see the Mills Family Farm truck.

'The burgers are amazing, Mia. Do you want one?'

I nodded absentmindedly. I didn't care what I ate as long as it was hot and there was plenty of it. I was impatient to read the strange letter in my pocket and explore the contents of the envelope. I needed to see what my mum had written.

Adam went to order our food and drinks as I slipped the letter from my jacket. The tattered page had been read multiple times, one of its corners torn and the paper flimsy to the touch.

I glanced up at Elizabeth who watched me with wide, eager eyes. She nodded her head as if I was waiting for her to tell me it was okay to carry on. I peeled open the page and began reading.

> *My dear Sebastian,*
>
> *I wish I had good news for you but I don't. I met with Joel and spoke about our situation. He was so cross when I explained that I'd made a mistake marrying Frank and that I wished to leave him and join you at the academy. His rage got out of hand and he hurt me. I'm scared, Se-*

bastian. Joel wouldn't let me leave. I tried every-
thing to convince him that this is where my heart
belongs, but he refused to listen. He believes that
the work you are doing is dangerous and instead
of loving you I should forget you exist.

I'm defying his orders by writing this letter
and I fear retribution should he discover we're
still in touch. Zak is growing suspicious although
he hasn't asked me outright. I'm so glad Mia is
too young to understand. I only hope that I can
persuade Zak to come to you instead of Joel when
the time comes. He is nearly sixteen so it's get-
ting close.

I believe in what you're doing, Sebastian, and
if it will save Zak and Mia from this fate and al-
low them to have a normal future, I hope you car-
ry on without me.

I'll try and write again soon but in the mean-
time know that I love you with all my heart and I
wish we could all be together.

Yours forever, C x

I stared at the paper for a long time, unable to think, move
or comprehend what it meant. Elizabeth's mouth hung open as
she struggled to find an appropriate response too.

Adam snapped us out of our stunned silence when he returned with three Diet Cokes.

'What have I missed?'

I handed him the letter and waited until he'd finished
reading. He let out a long, low whistle and passed it back.

'So your mum and Sebastian *were* a couple?'

'It certainly looks that way, but earlier, when I asked Sebastian if he had been having an affair with my mum, he said
no. He admitted to loving her but nothing else.'

'Who's Joel?' Adam cut in.

'Never heard that name before. He sounds like her boss or something, but that doesn't explain why Zak would go to him. Whoever this Joel is, he doesn't sound very nice.'

'How did he hurt your mother?' Elizabeth asked.

I skimmed over the letter once more. 'It doesn't say, but she was definitely scared. I wonder if he had something to do with her death.'

'I thought you said a werewolf killed your mum?'

'Yes, that's what it said on the file, and Sebastian confirmed it earlier. Maybe this Joel knew where they were and he took her to their lair. Do werewolves have lairs?'

Adam chuckled. 'I think they have three-bedroomed houses and attend church every Sunday.'

I groaned. I was more confused than ever.

A young waitress arrived with our food and gave us a cheery smile. The burger smelt good and my mouth started salivating before I could unwrap the cutlery from the napkin.

'What's in the envelope?' Elizabeth asked between mouthfuls.

I tugged the prize from my coat and tore it open. There was a single photograph inside, but this wasn't a pretty shot of my mum smiling or even a family portrait. My appetite disappeared as I studied the bare-chested boy chained to a laboratory table. He wore a shabby pair of trousers and dirty socks. With his arms and legs shackled, he strained against his restraints. A man in a long white lab coat was injecting something into the boy's upper thigh.

I covered my mouth with my free hand as a wave of nausea washed over me. The photograph was old, its colouring faded, but the anguish, fear and pain that distorted the boy's features were as raw as the day it was taken.

I flipped the photograph over and gasped. Printed in capitals on the reverse was *Prototype No. 0102.*

TEN

The next morning passed in a blur of one-on-one fitness training with Miss Ross and private tuition on a hastily erected
table under the picture window in Sebastian's office. I believed it was partly Sebastian's way of keeping a close eye on me
and partly his need to keep the student body safe from his homicidal niece. I alternated between reading and watching the distant woods with longing.

The sound of raised voices pulled my attention from my books
and I jumped out of my seat to investigate. Outside Sebastian's office window, partially obscured by shrubbery, stood a large, bald
man in an expensive-looking grey suit. He towered over Sebastian
by a good foot and a half and jabbed my uncle in the chest as he
enunciated every word.

'I. Want. Her. Gone.'

'Mr Parker, please. I assure you I have punished Miss Roberts
severely and...'

'I don't care if you threw her in the goddam animal cages, she
attacked my daughter and half killed her!'

I rolled my eyes at the exaggeration. Yes, Felicity looked like a ton of falling rocks had landed on her but 'half killed' was not even close.

'Mia is devastated over her actions. She was hoping to fit in at this academy after witnessing the brutal murder of her father—at the hands of a werewolf.'

The big man squared his shoulders and studied my uncle like he was a bug he'd just found in his dinner.

'I understand that your niece is damaged but that does NOT give her the right to...'

'I know, I know.' Sebastian raised his hands in submission. 'I beg you to let her complete her training, even if it's just to give her the basic skills she'll need to protect herself in later life.'

Mr Parker looked as if he was considering Sebastian's proposal, and I pressed myself closer to the window in anticipation of his response.

'Very well. She can fulfil her training, take the oath, and *then* I want her gone. If you fail to get rid of her, Dr Roberts, I shall have no other choice but to withdraw my funding.'

'There's no need for such a rash action, Mr Parker.'

'It took me a long time to find that tribe in Africa, Dr Roberts, and it took me even longer to find you. I needed a doctor qualified to use the tribe's knowledge to develop the serum. Do not make me begin my search again.'

Sebastian squirmed under the bald man's deadly glare.

'I assure you, sir, I am doing everything in my power to develop the correct transfusion. You will have your serum and the wolves will never need to turn or hunt again.'

I pressed my hand to my mouth. Was it possible that Sebastian was the person responsible for the screams I'd heard?

Felicity's father moved closer to Sebastian and spoke through clenched teeth.

OATH BREAKER

'I don't care about them turning, or hunting, because when this serum is ready, you, and your little band of hunters, will use it to destroy them all. For good.'

The door to Sebastian's office opened, making me jump and leap away from the window with a yelp. Miss Ross stuck her head in.

'You can take your lunch break now, Mia. Elizabeth is still sitting her science exam, but I think I saw Adam in the canteen.'

I didn't need telling twice and shot for the door, knocking the books and papers flying as I did. Miss Ross chuckled as I hurtled past her and headed towards the sounds of clattering plates.

'Hey!' Adam waved a hand in the air to attract my attention, and I headed towards him with my plate piled high.

'I'm starving,' I said.

'I can see that!' Adam's eyes twinkled as he laughed at my haste to eat. He had become as much of a friend to me as Elizabeth had. They were like a package deal. He clearly idolised her and therefore he got her friends as well.

'I'm going to sneak out later and see Cody.'

Adam showed no signs of surprise at hearing about my escape plans; he just shrugged his muscular shoulders.

'You need any help getting out?'

'Not if you leave your ladder at the window. I'll use that and keep to the shadows. I'll message Cody and tell him to meet me at the overhang at midnight.'

Adam nodded.

'What do you know about Felicity's dad?' I asked, recalling the conversation between him and Sebastian.

'Mr Parker? Not much. I know he's wealthy and travels all over the world visiting tribes and trading their knowledge of herbal medicine for western goods. I also know he despises werewolves. Why?'

'I've just overheard him and Sebastian talking and I don't think I've got a lot of time left. Mr Parker wants me out.'

'Well, if Mr Parker is anything like his daughter, I can't say I'm surprised. That family despise anyone who isn't like them.'

I nodded and stuffed a chip in my mouth.

'I was thinking, you might want to put your meeting with Cody off until tomorrow, Mia.' Adam wiggled his eyebrows at me.

'Huh?'

'I've got a present for you and you might need to use it as soon as possible so I can put it back before anyone realises it's gone.'

My eyes widened as he produced a small silver key from his pocket.

'You got it!'

'I got it,' he said, puffing his chest out with pride. 'But I need to return it fast. If the so-called store room *is* the entrance to a secret lab, someone will notice that this key is missing.'

I nodded and turned the object over and over in my hand.

'Okay, change of plan. We'll sneak into the lab tonight and I'll meet Cody tomorrow. I might just have something to tell him by then.'

I slipped the key into my jeans pocket. An odd feeling circled in the pit of my stomach and it wasn't indigestion. I'd heard a scream when I followed Felicity and her minion that night, and I didn't relish the thought of what we might find down there.

'I have a staff meeting tonight so I won't be able to come with you, but that also means Sebastian will be there too and not wandering around the school.'

'Perfect. That should give us time to do some snooping without worrying about the staff finding us.'

'I'll meet you back in your room when I'm done to make sure you're both back safely.'

I smiled up into Adam's handsome face, his mocha eyes twinkling under the fluorescent light. He'd wait to make sure

Elizabeth was safe, but I appreciated the gesture of including me in his thoughts.

I pushed my empty plate away and pressed my fingers against the pocket of my jeans, checking that the key was safe. Tonight we might have some answers. Tonight we might discover the truth.

·· ● ● ● ··

THE SCHOOL WAS in darkness as we crept down the main staircase and into the lobby. There were no lights on in Sebastian's office, the bolts were secured on the front doors and the canteen was silent for once.

Adam had told us the staff meeting was taking place in the library and to ensure that they weren't interrupted, a curfew had been set for the entire student body.

As we approached the store room door, I tried not to think about breaking school rules. Calming my nerves was top priority, but my hand shook slightly as I fished the key out of my pocket and pushed it into the lock. My scalp tingled with the anticipation of what we might discover.

The long corridor opened up beyond the stacks of paper and ink, and I gestured for Elizabeth to follow me. She secured the door behind us and rushed to my side.

Her clammy hand clutched at my elbow was strangely comforting. Adam had given us each a torch and we shone them across the grey walls until we found the stairwell leading down into the lab.

Elizabeth's eyes flashed with fear but she nodded at me to carry on, giving me the strength to place one foot on the top step and move down.

The staircase was made of stone and led to a large open room with a low ceiling. The floor was stained with dark splodges that looked to be years old. I tried not to think about where the stains had come from. At the back of the room, carved into the rock, was a large glass window and a steel door. We hugged the edge of the room as we made our way to the door, neither one of us wanting to walk over the dark marks that littered the concrete floor.

I grabbed the handle and pushed, relieved to find the door was unlocked and opened easily. The room was bright, white and clean, a contrast to the stone cavern we had left behind.

Locating the switch on the wall, I flicked it up, instantly flooding the area in a stark light from the fluorescent strips overhead. In the centre of the room was a silver trolley. I trailed a shaky hand across the shiny surface with a growing feeling of panic. The smell of antiseptic filled my senses, making me gag. Two leather straps connected to heavy chains hung from the metal gurney. Even though the straps had been recently sterilised, I could still see the muted red stains ingrained into the leather.

'What is this place?' whispered Elizabeth, her complexion ashen.

'Well, it's not the nurse's office.' My voice shook slightly as I offered my friend a weak smile.

Above the long metal bench that stretched across the length of the room was another large window. Through the glass, I could make out the dull shape of filing cabinets lining one wall.

'We need to get in there.' I stabbed my finger towards the window for Elizabeth's benefit as I made for the connecting door.

Turning the handle as I put my shoulder against the steel, I prayed that it wouldn't be locked. It gave with a loud squeak and we both froze to the spot and listened for any sound that someone had heard us. Silence. We walked inside.

In the far corner was yet another connecting door. It appeared that the underground lab consisted of single rooms leading off one another. Just how many rooms and what they all contained was a mystery. One that I might not be willing to discover tonight.

The filing cabinets were in alphabetical order and I went straight for R. Flicking through the tightly packed Manila files I found what I was looking for. Cassandra Roberts—my mother's file. I tucked it into the back of my jeans and pulled my hoodie down over the top to conceal my stolen goods. Elizabeth hissed and beckoned me over.

'Look at this one.'

She shone the torch over the worn label and I gasped. Written in bold pen was a single name—Joel Mills.

'Joel was the name in your mum's letter. Maybe it's the same guy.'

I nodded and took the file from her. Flipping open the front page, I found a brief summary sheet. Name, date of birth, family. My heart froze. There was a single name written under the title 'children': Cody Mills.

I couldn't stop my hands from shaking as I read the words. How could Cody be connected to a man who knew my mother? Knew her and hurt her. It had to be some mistake. Maybe a complete coincidence and not my Cody.

A noise just beyond the next door made me jump. Elizabeth grabbed at my arm and brandished the torch as a weapon. I was starting to wish we'd brought our staffs with us, even if purely for show.

We inched towards the steel door, keeping our backs to the row of filing cabinets. The bright light from the first room splashed long shadows across the floor.

'Are you going to open it?' Elizabeth's voice quivered in terror as I took hold of the handle. 'We don't know what's behind there. It could be a werewolf.'

Part of me wished it was. I'd come face-to-face with quite a few over the past couple of weeks and so far none of them had hurt me.

A rattle of chains and a low moan arose from beyond the door, which quickly reminded me of the screaming. Maybe whoever Felicity had been torturing was still here.

Drawing on all my resolve, I turned the handle and pushed the door wide.

OATH BREAKER

ELEVEN

Elizabeth froze next to me and I felt my own limbs lock into place preventing me from fleeing. I couldn't move or look away. The dark room smelt of blood, wet dog and something else, something I knew and loved. It was the scent of the woods. Earth, leaves, moss and the clean air. But it was tainted. Spoiled by the horror that we faced.

A man lay strapped to a long metal bed secured by two silver chains anchored into the concrete floor. Dried blood caked his upper torso and thin scars littered his skin. He wore tattered jeans but nothing else: no socks, shoes or T-shirt. His brown hair was long and scraggly, matted with blood.

'Oh my God!' Elizabeth let out a wracking sob as she pressed her hands to her face.

I took a tentative step forward and then another. Elizabeth whimpered behind me.

The man moaned again, a low keening sound. His head lolled to the right, and he opened his eyes to look straight at me. I gasped and stumbled backwards, bumping into a small silver stand covered with scalpels, needles and vials. They crashed to the floor as I sorted through my jumbled memories. A motorway service station. A mug of hot chocolate. Twinkling eyes full of mischief.

'Terry?' I stepped forward, my initial shock dissipating.

'You know him?' Elizabeth moved to my side and leant over the now motionless body.

'I met him on my way to Hood Academy, the night my dad was killed. I think he knows my brother.'

'What shall we do?' Elizabeth's voice had regained some composure, and it helped me calm the thumping sensation that flooded my ears and sucked all the moisture from my mouth.

'We have to get him out of here.'

'But how?'

I looked around the dank room. Apart from the metal bed and the tray of grotesque instruments, there was only a small stool. I hooked it up with my toe and flipped it upside down. Using one of the long, thin legs, I slid it inside the loop of Terry's chains near to where they attached to the floor. I twisted and twisted until the chain and the stool leg were tight, and then I twisted some more. Eventually, the chain link gave and snapped free. I moved to the other side and repeated my action.

With Terry now loose it was going to be up to Elizabeth and me to balance his weight and try to get him back through the rooms and up the stairs. It seemed an impossible task.

'Where are we going to take him? We can't exactly hide him in our room?' I dabbed at a cut on Terry's lip with my sleeve and he groaned. Elizabeth flinched.

'We can take him to Adam's room,' she suggested. 'It's on the ground floor next to the library, and he's got access to the lawns. Maybe we can hide him until he's strong enough to make a run for the woods.'

I mulled this plan over, nodding in agreement.

'We'll get him upstairs and then you can try and get a message to Adam. We need his help to carry Terry the rest of the way,' I said. 'We must get him out of that meeting somehow.'

'Okay, I'll try.'

Terry coughed and rolled onto his side. His eyes found mine again and I tried to give him a reassuring smile.

'Terry, it's me, Mia. This is my friend, Elizabeth. We're going to help you.'

He nodded and tried to sit up. Whatever drug was pumping around his system clearly affected his coordination as he would have fallen to the ground if I hadn't stopped him. I hooked my arm around his shoulders and winced at the heat of his body. He was burning up.

We helped him swing his legs off the trolley and stood on either side of him as he tentatively tested the power in his limbs. Although very shaky, he was able to hold his own weight with a little help from us. We threaded our way through the maze of rooms. Elizabeth stopped to scoop up the information on Joel Mills before exiting the files room and closing the door behind us.

The concrete stairs were much harder to navigate. Terry had little strength left by the time we reached them.

He slid down the cold stone wall and sat on the bottom step with a defeated slump to his shoulders.

'Go get Adam,' I said to Elizabeth. 'Be careful and stay hidden.'

Elizabeth gave me a tight smile, shot a glance at Terry and then bolted off up the stairs, her torch light bouncing off the walls.

I knelt on the ground in front of the crumpled boy and stroked his hair away from his face. When I last saw him, he had been so full of life and energy, with a cheeky smile and a confidence that I could only dream of. I felt a heavy weight pressing down on my chest as I looked at him now.

'What happened to you?'

He lifted his gaze and gave me a weak smile.

'Captured. Tortured,' he whispered.

Tears threatened to fall and I blinked them away and carried on stroking his face. He reminded me so much of Zak. I knew now wasn't the right time to ask, but I couldn't help myself.

'Do you know where my brother is?'

Terry dropped his gaze and licked his parched lips. I wished I had a bottle of water I could give him.

'Yes,' he said eventually, his voice hoarse. 'He's here, in Ravenshood.'

I thought my heart might explode with joy at hearing his words. My breath caught in my throat and a million questions bubbled to the surface, but before I could ask any of them, I heard footsteps above us.

The blood in my veins ran cold as I recognised Felicity's voice.

'The beast has been moved to the interrogation lab,' she said, 'but it just means we've got more knives to play with.'

Her sadistic laugh ricocheted off the stone walls and circled my throat like a noose. I had to move Terry. It would be catastrophic if she made it down the stairs and found us.

'Can you stand?' I whispered, urging Terry to his feet.

He grasped my arm for support and leant heavily against the wall. I noticed the smear of blood he left on the stone from his wounds.

My mouth felt like a sandpit, and yet the moisture that trickled down my spine did nothing to offer any refreshment.

I spun around looking for somewhere to hide, then I spotted a darkened alcove beyond the stairwell. It housed a mop and bucket and a janitor's uniform.

I shoved Terry without any preamble into the shadows and wrapped the grey uniform around his bare shoulders.

Felicity and her three friends reached the store room just as I melted into the alcove, my back to Terry, pushing him into the tiny space.

'You gonna let me have a go at torturing the monster tonight, Flic?' said Elena Fields, one of Felicity's longest-serving squad members, pushing herself to the front of the group.

'I suppose you deserve to have a go,' Felicity said, standing by the connecting door to the bright room. 'Just remember, we can't kill him. He might be disgusting vermin, but he's vital to Dr Roberts's work.'

I flinched at the mention of Sebastian's involvement. I hadn't wanted to believe it when I overheard him talking to Felicity's father. I knew he was doing something, creating some kind of serum, but I hadn't believed he was capable of torture.

The girls moved off into the other room, the door clicking shut behind them. I let the breath I'd been holding in rush out in one go.

'Come on, we've got to move.'

I supported Terry the best I could as we made slow progress up the stairs. It wouldn't take Felicity long to discover that Terry was missing.

We reached the stock room just as I heard raised voices coming from the bottom of the stairs. I pushed Terry out of the door, and we crashed straight into a large man blocking the exit.

I recoiled before noticing the kind eyes peering down at me.

'Oh, thank goodness. Adam, we've got to move. Felicity is right behind us.'

Adam wrapped his arm around Terry's back and manoeuvred him across the foyer and out of sight. I followed, hearing the stock room door burst open just as I escaped from view.

We hurried down the dark corridor until we arrived at a brown door with a number seven painted on it. Adam knocked once, then twice in sharp succession. The door opened and Elizabeth peeked out. She moved out of the way to allow Adam room to carry Terry through.

'Are you okay?' Elizabeth grabbed my hand and squeezed it as I entered Adam's bedroom.

'That was too close. Felicity turned up with her rent-a-torturer crew. I didn't think we'd make it.'

I flopped into a chair by the patio doors and stared out at the inky blackness. My heart was still pumping like crazy and I shoved my hands under my legs to stop them shaking.

'Is he going to be okay?' I asked Adam, who was settling Terry into the bed.

'Most of the surface wounds are already healing, but the drugs he's been given may take a while longer to come out of his system.'

Terry mumbled something and I moved over to the bed, sitting next to him and taking his hand.

'You're safe now, Terry.'

'The pack,' he said. 'He wants the pack, your uncle. It's my pack he wants.'

With that he slipped into a deep sleep. Gentle snores filled the room as Adam, Elizabeth and I looked on in shock.

'What if Felicity raises the alarm?' Elizabeth asked, her voice nothing more than a faint quiver.

I shook my head. 'She won't want to risk exposing herself and what she's been doing. She might be working on my uncle's behalf, but I'm not sure he knows about her cruel extracurricular activity. Terry should be safe here until the morning, and hopefully he'll have regained his strength by then.'

'I'll replace the key first thing tomorrow,' Adam said, moving to Elizabeth's side and wrapping a protective arm around her shoulder. 'You two need to act as casual as possible.'

'Casual? You mean not own up to breaking into a secret lab, stealing confidential files and rescuing a werewolf?'

That's right—a werewolf. Terry was a werewolf.

Adam grinned. 'Precisely.'

'I've never seen a werewolf in its human form.' Elizabeth's soft voice floated across the room.

'Cody told me they are as human as you or me, but I guess I wasn't expecting them to be people we know.'

'What are you going to do now?' Adam asked.

It was a simple enough question, but if I was being honest with myself, I had no clue what to do next.

'All we can do is wait for Terry to recover and see if he can give us any answers. He's a werewolf, with a pack that's clearly in danger, but he also knows where my brother is.'

'And what about the fact that Cody's dad might have had something to do with your mum's death?' Elizabeth whispered.

I rested my elbows on my knees and allowed my head to drop. Where the hell should I start?

'I promised Cody that I'd meet him and keep him up to date on any news.'

'Well, you've certainly got news to share with him. Do you think he knows Terry too?'

I couldn't think about that because if Cody *did* know Terry, that meant he probably knew Zak. I didn't think I could face it if anyone else was lying to me.

'What do you think Dr Roberts is going to do when he finds out Terry is gone?'

I stared at the silhouettes of leaves dancing across the floor. Sebastian was going to flip out when he discovered the werewolf was gone, but I wouldn't like to guess at what he would do if he knew it was me who helped it escape.

'I don't know,' I said quietly. 'I'm sure we'll find out soon enough.'

$$\cdot\cdot\bullet\,\bullet\,\bullet\cdot\cdot$$

I TAPPED LIGHTLY on the office door as I pushed it open. My books were pressed into my chest as I hugged them close, using them as a shield against any impending danger. Sebastian sat behind his desk staring into a coffee cup. He didn't acknowledge my entrance.

I dropped into the chair at my table by the window and began unloading my pens and paper. The rustling of pages roused Sebastian from his stupor and he glanced around the room, noticing me for the first time. There were dark circles under his bloodshot eyes and stubble dusted his square jaw.

'Sorry, Mia, I didn't hear you come in.'

I smiled and flipped open one of my textbooks. 'That's okay, you looked...busy.'

His attention slid back to the coffee cup and he resumed his staring. My stomach churned as I wondered about the reason for his apparent lack of energy. By now, he must know that the werewolf was gone, but instead of the explosion of anger that I had expected, he looked defeated, broken and lost. I felt a sudden pang of sorrow for my uncle.

'Are you okay?' I couldn't help myself. I needed to know.

He lifted his head and looked across at me, his gaze drifting over my head and settling beyond the window and on the distant woods.

'All my work, those long years of hard study, all for nothing.'

'What do you mean?'

He stood up and scratched at his unshaven chin, carrying on as if I hadn't spoken.

'Take the day off, Mia. Go do teenage girl stuff with your friends.'

He pushed a small button on a control panel built into his desk and a speaker system crackled to life.

'Due to unforeseen circumstances, all classes will be cancelled today. All students have the day off.'

Through the heavy wooden door, I could hear the cheers and cries from the rest of the students and a thunderous clatter of feet as everyone dashed for their rooms or escaped out of the front doors hoping that the head of the academy wouldn't change his mind.

I collected my things, keeping a wary eye on Sebastian as he braced his hands against the edge of his desk, his head hung low.

'Can I get you anything?'

Sebastian shook his head and turned to face the bookshelves and the many photo frames that held images of my mother. I scooped up my books as quickly as I could and edged towards the door.

'I'll see you tomorrow.'

He didn't answer.

•• ● ••

I RAN UPSTAIRS, dodging the masses of excited students who didn't know what to make of their impromptu day off. Elizabeth arrived back at our room just after me and we both dumped our books, changed into jeans and jumpers and darted back down the stairs.

'What have you decided to do with your day, girls?' Miss Ross blocked the head of the corridor leading to Adam's room. She wore a light turquoise running top and stretchy black joggers. 'Fancy joining me for a run?'

I screwed my face up as I thought about the last run I'd gone on. The only pleasant part of it was meeting Cody.

Elizabeth was faster with a reply. 'Sorry, miss, we're heading to the library. I want to show Mia the mythology section.'

'Excellent idea, Elizabeth. There's plenty to keep you busy in there.' With that, she jogged off across the foyer and out into the bright sunshine.

'That was quick thinking, Lizzie.'

She grinned at me and nodded at the sign hanging from the ceiling. The painted wood was starting to peel but the word 'Library' was still very clear.

We rushed along the corridor until we reached the nondescript brown door with the number seven painted on it in wobbly lettering.

The door opened a crack when we knocked but was swung wide when Adam saw it was us. Elizabeth darted forward to fling her arms around his neck and I nodded my hello as I squeezed past my friends.

Terry was sitting up in Adam's bed looking much better than he had last night. He had showered and was wearing one of Adam's navy T-shirts, which highlighted the twinkle in his eyes. He grinned as I approached.

'Mia!'

'Hello, Terry. How are you feeling?'

I perched on the edge of the bed and folded my hands in my lap. He watched my every movement.

'I'm doing okay, thanks. Your friend will make a fine doctor if he ever gets bored of gardening.' He laughed and it rumbled from deep inside his chest.

I couldn't help but smile up at him. When I'd met him on the night my dad was brutally murdered, I never thought our paths would cross again, even though he had left me with cryptic clues and warnings. Yet here he was, a werewolf in human form, lounging in my friend's bedroom.

'You want to know about Zak, don't you?' He lowered his voice and lay a big calloused hand over mine. 'It's okay to ask me about him.'

I couldn't hold back the tears as they tumbled down my cheeks, hot and sticky. Terry pulled me closer and I nestled in the crook of his arm like *he* was my big brother and could protect me from the world.

'Zak never left you, not really. He had to move out so he could discover who he was, but he understood that you needed protecting, so he assigned some *friends* to check in on you every now and then. I was one of those friends.'

'What do you mean by he *had* to move out? Was it because of our dad? He should have taken me with him when he went.'

'You were far too young, Mia. Where he was going, it was too dangerous for you.'

'I don't understand. What could be so dangerous that he couldn't take his kid sister along? Where did he go?'

Terry tightened his hold around me and leant his head back against the wall. I spotted Elizabeth and Adam move closer to the bed as they listened to Terry's story.

'He needed to find Joel, the pack leader. He was sixteen and the time had come to commit to his family.'

'Pack leader? I don't understand. Did he go after Joel for hurting our mother? If Zak's a hunter too then surely he could have told me.'

Terry shook his head slowly. 'Your brother isn't a hunter, Mia. He's a werewolf. Just like your mum.'

TWELVE

My world spun away from me. I was aware that strong, warm arms were holding me, and I could hear the soothing tones of Elizabeth's voice in the background, but the noise in my head was terrifying.

'Are you absolutely sure?' Elizabeth asked Terry, her hand placed protectively on my shoulder.

'Of course I'm sure. We've been friends for ten years. I should know if my best friend is a werewolf.'

I pushed myself upright and felt instantly chilled as I untangled myself from Terry's arms. Elizabeth's hand remained on my shoulder, her way of telling Terry that I was *her* best friend and no-one was going to mess with either of us.

'How?' It was all I could ask.

My brain couldn't comprehend the magnitude of Terry's revelation and the number of questions that bubbled up inside me.

Terry gazed down into my eyes and I noticed a kindness there. He didn't want to hurt me or frighten me. Apart from Elizabeth and Adam, he was the only one who had been honest with me from the start.

'How is my brother a werewolf?'

'It's hereditary,' he said, studying my reaction. 'Your mother was a werewolf, as was her father and his mother, and so on.'

I stored this genealogical insight for later and turned to Elizabeth.

'You told me that a person has to have the sight to become a hunter. I *saw* a werewolf kill my father and that's why Sebastian brought me here. I'm a hunter.'

Elizabeth nodded. 'It's true...or so I was told.'

We both looked at Terry for confirmation.

'In every pack, a cub is born, which unleashes the hunter to protect and serve...'

I jumped off the bed, holding my hand out to silence Terry, and began pacing the floor. 'Don't start quoting Dr Neale to me. I've read his dreary little book and nowhere in there does it say anything about siblings hunting each other.'

'Whoa! Who said anything about hunting each other?'

I stared at Terry with my mouth hanging wide open and the best 'duh' expression I could muster spread across my face.

'I'm a hunter. Zak's a werewolf. You do the math!'

'Mia, there's a reason you can see werewolves and it's not because you sparked the hunter gene. You come from a family of werewolves.'

Elizabeth gasped and took an involuntary step away from me.

'What is it?' I asked her.

She dropped onto the bed, her face as pale as the moon. Although she was looking at me, she was talking to Terry. 'When will she turn?'

'Turn? What are you talking about? Lizzie, who will turn?'

All eyes settled on me and I froze.

'I'm not a werewolf,' I said, but the tremor in my voice betrayed my doubt.

'It's okay, we'll work it out between us.' Elizabeth was at my side before I slid down the wall of Adam's room and curled up into a foetal position.

•• • ● • ••

I MANAGED TO escape the overly protective embrace of my best friend and disappear into Adam's small bathroom. I could hear the voices of my friends waft under the door as they analysed my family history, future options and moon cycles.

Staring at my face in the mirror, I tried to picture how I would look as a wolf. My hair was dark brown like Zak's and curled over my shoulders. Did that mean I'd look like one of those Scottish long-haired cows? I groaned and pulled at my top lip—was that a fang?

There was a soft tap at the bathroom door and Elizabeth's gentle voice pulled me back from studying my fingernails— had they grown in the last hour?

'I'm fine, Lizzie,' I whispered, although if I was brutally honest, I didn't think I'd ever be fine again.

I opened the door and swept my gaze across the room. Terry was sitting up on the bed, the shape of his strong muscles visible beneath his borrowed shirt. He gave a short nod of his head as I caught his eye. Adam stood close by watching me with a crooked smile, and Elizabeth was eager to grasp my hand and squeeze my fingers. They looked just the same as they always did. No horror, fear or judgement in their eyes, just love and friendship.

'How are you not freaking out about this?' I asked Elizabeth and Adam.

Adam wrapped his arms around his torso. 'I have a confession,' he said. 'I've been around werewolves all my life, Mia. I knew Miss Ross when she worked at the academy down in Cornwall, and it was on her recommendation that I got the job here.'

'How didn't I know about that?'

Elizabeth shrugged her delicate shoulders. 'Sorry, Mia. I only just found out myself, but I should have told you.'

'It sounds like your teacher was getting all the players in place before you arrived,' Terry said.

'What do you mean?'

Elizabeth pulled me across the room and sat us both down on the bed next to Terry.

'Don't you find it all a bit odd?' she asked. 'Miss Ross brought Adam here just before you arrived.'

'Yes, and it was Miss Ross who suggested Elizabeth as a roommate for you,' Adam added.

'But Miss Ross couldn't know I was coming here. Nobody knew until the last minute. My dad was killed and within hours Sebastian turned up. It all happened so fast.'

'Mia, I wasn't the first of my pack to be captured and tortured. I'm just one in a long line.'

'You're the first to escape,' added Adam with a soft laugh.

Terry grinned. 'I am indeed. Despite the drugs, knives and questions, I never gave in. I never told them what they wanted to know.'

A chill crept along my spine as I listened to his words and imagined the horrors he had endured.

'What did they want to know?'

'Your uncle was only interested in our pack. He wanted Zak above everything else.'

'Is that why they captured you? To get to Zak?'

'I was careless. After our meeting at the service station I followed you here. I watched from the treeline to see if you'd been taken to the laboratory too, but when I saw you training with all your hunter friends, I knew I had to tell your brother.'

'What did he say?'

'I never made it. I got too close to the school and didn't see the attack coming. I was taken to the lab and stayed there until you found me.'

'So, if you didn't report back to Zak, does he even know that I'm here? Does he think I'm the enemy?'

Terry shook his head. 'I'm not the only one keeping an eye out for you, Mia. Don't worry.'

I thought about all the times I'd imagined someone was watching me and shivered. It was creepy rather than comforting.

'What if Miss Ross knew what was going to happen?' Elizabeth asked.

I swallowed the bile that rose up like a tsunami threatening to roar from deep within my throat.

'You think she was behind the attack on my dad?'

Adam knelt in front of me. 'No, she couldn't have been. I've known her my entire life and she would never cause *you* any harm.'

'Me? Wouldn't cause me any harm? Why just me?'

'Adam?' Elizabeth's brow creased as she watched her boyfriend splutter for the right words. 'What aren't you telling us?'

'Miss Ross...and your mother, they were best friends from a young age.'

Both Elizabeth and I sucked in a deep breath.

Adam continued. 'Just before your mum died, she asked Miss Ross to keep an eye on you. To bring you here if you were ever in any danger. Miss Ross recruited me to look out for you too.'

I noticed the hurt flicker across Elizabeth's face at Adam's revelation and felt relieved that I wasn't the only one he'd kept in the dark.

'That doesn't explain how she knew about my dad's murder before it even happened.'

'Maybe she has contacts with the werewolves.'

We all turned to Terry looking for confirmation.

He threw his hands in the air. 'Maybe. I don't know who Zak is in touch with outside the pack. We're brothers, not a married couple.'

I stood up and began pacing the small floor space.

'It's like she *wants* you to know the truth.' Terry said. 'Bringing in her own team.' He nodded towards Adam who was trying to placate Elizabeth. 'And ensuring you had a friend here to support you.'

I thought about it for a moment, and it started to make sense. Of all the hundreds of students in the school, why put me with Elizabeth? She was light and full of energy and passion. I was dark, moody and broken. We were at the furthest ends of the friendship spectrum, and yet I couldn't imagine my life without Elizabeth in it. She'd helped me to see the spark of a life that flickered deep inside my gut. Miss Ross had made that happen.

'But why does Miss Ross want me to know the truth?'

Elizabeth shrugged her shoulders. 'Maybe it's a way of repaying a debt or some strange bond between hunter and werewolf—her and your mum.'

I chuckled at Elizabeth's observation. 'A bit like us, you mean?'

She smiled and her bright blue eyes sparkled.

'No matter how hairy you get, I'll always be your roomie.'

'Hey!' I thumped her on the arm as she darted away from me laughing. She hid behind Adam, who circled his arms behind him in a mock attempt to protect her. He was clearly forgiven.

Terry stood up from the bed, towering above all of us. I didn't remember him being so tall last night.

'As much fun as it is to debate the inner workings of the minds of Hood Academy's teaching staff, I need to get back to my pack and let them know I'm alive.'

He made for the patio doors and the rest of us rushed to block his path.

'The entire student body is roaming the campus at the moment. If you step outside, you'll be seen and reported. Or worse, recaught.'

Adam nodded in agreement. 'Mate, you *look* like an escaped werewolf and some of these girls are itching for a fight.'

My thoughts turned to Felicity and what she would do if she discovered that Terry was hiding in the gardener's bedroom.

'Adam's right,' I said. 'Let me go meet my friend, Cody. He might be able to help me locate your pack and get word to them. Once that's done, we'll break you out when it gets dark.' I pulled out my phone and sent Cody a quick message.

Terry cocked his head to the side and considered me for a moment.

'What?'

'How do you know Cody?'

'Never mind how *I* know Cody, how do *you* know him?'

'He's my brother!'

The silence was so overwhelming, even the insects in the garden behind us held their breath.

'How is that possible?'

'Well, he's a foster brother. His folks took me in years ago along with a few other kids and we've stuck together ever since.'

'So you're one of the loud brothers he told me about.'

Terry nodded his head and gave me a goofy grin.

'Does he know you're a werewolf?'

'He found out a long time ago and he's...cool about it.'

I nodded, stunned by this admission. Cody knew his brother was a werewolf. Maybe that explained his initial reaction when I mentioned Hood Academy at our first meeting. He was concerned for his family, not the town. I turned towards the door but Terry stopped me, tugging at my sleeve until I was facing him, a sly smile twitching at the corner of his mouth.

'Why did you blush when I mentioned Cody's name?'

I knew he was teasing me, but I couldn't stop the additional burn as it shot up my neck and coloured my cheeks. I stuck my middle finger up at him and flung the patio door open.

'I'll see you all later.'

I could hear them all laughing as I stomped off across the grass.

·· • ● • ··

THE SUN WAS high in the sky as I reached the overhang, and a cool breeze ruffled the luscious green patchwork of leaves overhead. Cody wasn't there when I arrived but I knew he wouldn't be long.

I pulled my mum's Manila file from my bag and flipped through the pages of notes inside. I was still shocked at the discovery she had been a werewolf. One of the sheets in her file detailed the infection she had contracted from a werewolf bite. Was that how Joel hurt her? Had the pack leader bitten her?

Someone had scrawled a page of notes detailing the injection dose and dates of administration. Beneath this, in Sebastian's neat handwriting, were some footnotes, added like a journal entry.

> *Unfortunately, I was unable to stabilise the serum for prototype 0102. It appears the dosage was lethal to the subject. Several modifications were made, and it is my belief that prototype 0118 may be working. The werewolf gene is diminished slightly.*

I digested the words as a growing sensation of dread pooled in my gut. On the surface, the idea was a good one. It meant that no human being would have to go through the pain of turning every full moon. But the idea that Sebastian tested his serum on my mum knotted my insides. The thought of Terry chained to the steel trolley in the cold, dark basement steamrolled through my brain. Had Sebastian chained my mum to the same gurney?

I pulled the other file from my bag, and the tattered label with Joel Mills written on it gleamed in the sunlight. Near the

SHELLEY WILSON

back of the folder was a colour photograph of a young couple. They were smiling and had their arms circling each other. It was a happy image, full of joy and love.

'Why do you have that?'

I jumped at the sound of Cody's voice close behind me and dropped the picture back into the file.

'You scared me.' I held a palm up to my chest as if trying to stuff my heart back into my ribcage.

'That photo...it's of my parents.'

I blinked up at the wide-eyed boy who stood over me, his blonde hair dulled by the halo of sunlight that burnt behind him.

So the file was right. Joel Mills was Cody's father. I wasn't sure how to break the news that his dad might have killed my mum, but as I looked up at his sorrowful eyes, I knew I couldn't hurt him like that.

He dropped down to sit beside me and held his hand out for the file. I gave it to him without a sound. From what I'd read on the opening page, Joel and Pauline Mills were not killed in a car accident as Cody believed. I could relate to the shock of discovering the lies, having found out that my own mum hadn't died in an accident. I needed Cody to know the truth, however hard it might be.

'If it helps, they lied to me about how my mum died too.'

His blue eyes found mine and my heart almost broke at the pain I saw there.

'I thought...' He shook his head, his chest heaving as he struggled with the emotions churning inside of him.

'I know.' It was all I could say. I understood his pain only too well.

I reached out and took his warm hand. I had so much to ask him, but I didn't know where to begin.

'You were right about the academy,' I said softly.

His head hung low as he hunched over the photo of his parents, his blonde hair gleaming in the sunshine. At the sound of my voice, he lifted his gaze to meet mine.

'They are doing experiments on people...werewolves,' I added. 'We rescued someone last night and we're keeping him safe until nightfall.'

Cody just watched me, not making a sound or rushing me to fill in the blanks for him.

I took a deep breath and blurted out the rest. 'It's your brother, Terry.'

I don't know what I'd been expecting him to do on hearing the news but sitting in silence and watching the coming and goings in the valley below wasn't it.

'Did you hear me?' I asked, my voice rising slightly. 'Your brother was being tortured in the basement of my school and I saved him.'

Nothing.

I collected the files and thought about snatching the photo of Joel and Pauline from Cody's hand but decided against it. Stuffing everything into my bag, I got to my feet and dusted off my jeans. Cody still hadn't moved or reacted to my news.

Giving him one last look, I uttered an exasperated sigh before storming off into the trees.

I'd almost made it back to the academy when I heard his heavy footsteps running behind me.

'Mia, stop!'

I whirled around to face him, clenching my fists as I watched him approach. I had risked a lot to save his brother and he was being ungrateful and infuriating.

'I'm sorry,' he said as he stopped in front of me. 'It was such a shock seeing that photo and finding out that the academy had something to do with my parents' death. I wasn't thinking straight. What you've done, for Terry, and me... My family mean the world to me.'

'I know they do,' I said. 'So do mine.'

He moved a step closer and took hold of my hands.

'I haven't been totally honest with you, Mia.'

I held my breath; this was the moment he either told me that he knew his dad had hurt my mum or that he was fully aware of Terry's full-moon activities.

'My brothers and sisters, the ones that were saved by my parents, they are my family, no matter what blood flows in their veins. Terry, Byron, Sean, Jenna, Katy and...Zak.'

I stared at him for a long moment, aware that I'd heard his words but unable to process them and sort them into a suitable emotional category. Zak? My Zak? So he did know him.

'Your brother came to live with us when I was seven, long before my parents were killed. He became part of my family straight away and my dad helped him through...certain changes.'

My voice sounded tinny and distant when I finally spoke. 'I'm fully aware of the changes my brother had to go through. Terry filled me in on the whole werewolf DNA that runs in the family. What I want to know is did you know who I was when we met?'

Cody dropped my hands and they swung through the vast void that separated us even though we were only a few steps apart.

'Yes,' he whispered. 'After I saw you in the woods that night, I wanted to meet you in person but I didn't know how I could. Going anywhere near the academy is dangerous for us, so I...'

I held my hand up to silence him.

'When did you see me for the first time, Cody?'

'It was the night you ran away. You came crashing through the trees and we had to investigate the sound, so Zak led us to the overhang. You were leaning against a tree trunk looking really sad. Then you saw us.'

I gasped and pushed my fingers to my lips. The four wolves in the forest.

'You...you're a werewolf?'

I mentally kicked myself. Now I thought about it, he was part of a random family that included Terry and Zak—werewolves. How had I not put the pieces together? Even after Terry told me Cody was cool about his brother being a wolf, it still never dawned on me that he was one too. Or perhaps I hadn't wanted to believe it.

Cody nodded, his blonde hair flopping into his eyes until he brushed it away. I watched his hair dance in the sunlight and thought back to that night. A large brown wolf had broken away and circled me. Was that Zak? There was another wolf too, its fur golden and its eyes as blue as the ocean.

'Oh my God.' My knees gave way and I dropped to the dirt track with a thud. Cody rushed to my side.

'I'm so sorry, Mia. Zak told me to stay away from you and the academy, but I couldn't. I had to meet you and speak with you.'

'All this time and you knew about the werewolves, my brother and me. Did Byron know who I was that day in the café?'

'Not until you told him your name. When we're in wolf form we don't really see you in the same way as when we're human. The scent is the same, but you were scared that night in the woods. You just smelt of cinnamon in the café.' His voice trailed off as he caught my mortified expression.

'So why hasn't Zak come for me?' That hurt more than the lies. My brother knew where I was, had always known where I was, but remained in the shadows—or in his wolf form. I felt abandoned all over again.

'When my parents died, Zak became the alpha wolf. He has to be careful. Coming anywhere near Hood Academy is more dangerous for him because of your uncle. It's like he has a personal vendetta against our pack. He suspected that Terry was being held here, but we couldn't do anything about it.'

'So you used me. You sent me to free him instead of getting your hands dirty.'

'I'm so sorry, Mia. I never wanted to put you in danger. Neither did Zak. He's spent his life trying to keep you safe and prepare for your future.'

Tears spilt down my cheeks as I sat in the dirt trying to digest Cody's words, but they stuck in my throat.

'But I wasn't safe,' I cried. 'I was never safe. Our father beat me until I couldn't see, he hurt me so I couldn't walk and he terrorised me every day of my life. Zak didn't keep me safe. He left me to rot.'

I jumped up, grabbing my bag as I did, and ran past the old animal cages and across the lawns, wiping frantically at the tears that flowed down my face with the back of my sleeve.

I stumbled through Adam's patio doors and collapsed in a heap on the floor, sobbing hysterically until Terry scooped me up and set me down on the bed. He stroked my hair until I felt the tears subside and the ache in my heart lessen.

'I'm guessing you spoke to Cody.'

I nodded and blew my nose on the tissue Adam handed me.

'Yes, he told me everything. How he's a werewolf too and that Zak's your pack leader.' I hiccupped as the sobs wracked through me. 'Zak chose his pack over me, Terry. I'm not sure I can ever forgive him for that. And now, I'm all alone. Again.'

THIRTEEN

We spread the contents of the files across both beds. I propped my mother's photograph on my pillow. It gave me a warm feeling in the pit of my stomach, like she was there with me, trying to sort out the lies from the evidence in front of us.

'Terry said he was sorry.' Elizabeth had only just returned from Adam's room. The night was dark and overcast and Terry had made his escape, running for the treeline wearing one of Adam's navy hoodies and joggers.

'I'm not interested. Zak, Cody and all his pack of werewolves can rot in hell for all I care.' Of course, I didn't really mean that. I was just so angry at all of them. Mad at Cody for not telling me the truth from the beginning, cross with Terry because he could have given me more than cryptic clues at our first meeting, and as for Zak—I was furious at my brother for everything. I'd believed in him and he'd let me down.

Elizabeth gave a little half laugh in response and carried on reading through the file on Joel Mills. She had been nothing but supportive since I returned to our shared room with puffy eyes and incoherent babble about renegade siblings.

I wondered if it was possible to adopt Elizabeth as my sister and trade off a hairy, slobbering man-wolf. A giggle escaped my lips and Elizabeth raised a single eyebrow.

'Something funny?'

I shook my head. 'Not at all. That's why I'm laughing. My entire life has fallen apart in a matter of weeks, and now I discover I'm descended from werewolves.'

We both giggled. Then we laughed out loud. It wasn't long until we were rolling around the floor, clutching our sides and wiping away the tears that fell. It felt so good to have fun.

After we had exhausted all inappropriate humour, we sat with our backs against the wall and stared at the mass of photographs and graphs that littered the room.

'Do we even know what we're looking for?'

I hiccupped a little and shook my head. 'Not a clue.'

'Okay, let's look at what we do know.' Elizabeth clambered up from the floor and stood over the mountain of paper with her hands on her slim hips.

'We know that your mum was a werewolf and that Joel was the pack leader. We assume from her letter to Sebastian that your mum was a member of Joel's pack and he didn't let her leave.'

I stood up and adopted the same stance as Elizabeth. Surveying the yellowed pages, I processed Elizabeth's findings and voiced some additional thoughts that had been brewing in my mind for a while.

'Terry says that once you're sworn in as a pack member you can't leave without good reason. Apparently, falling in love with a werewolf hunter was frowned upon in Joel's pack.'

Elizabeth laughed.

'We now know that my brother is a werewolf and abandoned me to join Joel's pack after Mum died.'

Elizabeth snatched up the crumpled letter we found behind my mum's photograph in Sebastian's office and opened it up.

'Your mum wanted Zak to come to Sebastian and not Joel. Why? What could your uncle offer Zak that a werewolf pack leader couldn't?'

'Freedom.'

Neither of us had noticed Miss Ross slip inside the room, nor did we hear her creep up on us.

We squealed in unison as she spoke.

'So it *was* you two who helped our guest to leave.' She wasn't asking. The glint in her eye told me she knew exactly what we'd been up to.

A sharp tug of fear pulled at my gut.

'Don't worry, I'm not going to tell Sebastian. Believe it or not, girls, I'm on your side.'

She stared down at the papers strewn across the bed, and I noticed the small muscle in her jaw twitching. If she had information but didn't know if she should tell us, it was down to us to coax it out of her. Miss Ross could have a vital clue from her friendship with my mum and her working relationship with Sebastian.

'We didn't mean any harm,' Elizabeth said, her voice barely a whisper.

'Oh, I know you didn't.' Miss Ross patted Elizabeth's hand and the warmth returned to her eyes as she turned to look at me.

'I wanted you to know the truth about your mother, Mia. No child should be left in the dark about their heritage. Your mother was a kind, caring and beautiful woman, and she was my dearest friend. I felt obliged to point you in the right direction. It was obvious that Sebastian was never going to tell you.'

'So you hired Adam to help you out.'

'Kind of,' she said. 'I've known Adam a long time and when I asked for his assistance he was only too happy to come to Hood Academy. I needed someone I could trust on the inside to watch out for you without arousing suspicion. Adam fit that role perfectly.' She moved around the bed, glancing at the collection of evidence. 'When young Elizabeth here had her altercation with Felicity, it presented me with another way of keeping a closer eye on you.'

I balked and instinctively took a step away from Elizabeth. Her eyes widened.

'No! I didn't know anything about that, I promise.'

'Relax, Mia. Elizabeth was as clueless to my plans as you were. I just felt it would be advantageous for the two of you to be friendly, so I persuaded Sebastian to put you together as roommates.'

My initial panic subsided as I moved to stand beside my friend once more.

'I'm sorry,' I said quietly.

She smiled and reached for my hand.

Miss Ross continued, 'It all worked out quite well when Adam was dazzled by Elizabeth before you arrived.'

Elizabeth blushed and lowered her head.

'Oh, don't worry, my dear. Young love is a wonderful thing and I wouldn't do anything to harm your relationship.'

'Did you help Adam to get the key to the underground lab?' I asked, trying to work out how Adam had helped Miss Ross when he had seemed as much in the dark as the rest of us.

Miss Ross chuckled and took a seat on the end of Elizabeth's bed, pushing the pages of Joel Mills's file to the side. Her eyes were bright and sparkled in the light cast from the table lamp.

'No, I only told Adam to befriend you. I didn't give him any more information than that. I thought it would be a slow task with everything you had been through at home. But it appears that you girls, and Adam, discovered far more than I had planned all by yourselves.' She fiddled with the hem of Elizabeth's blanket as if choosing her next words carefully. 'I merely wanted you to learn that your mother was a werewolf so you could prepare yourself for the change should you carry the gene. But you dug a little deeper and unearthed Hood Academy's secrets.'

'I think you're giving us too much credit, miss. We might have found my uncle's files and the hidden lab, but none of us have any clue what it all means.'

I grabbed a file from Elizabeth's bed and waved it in the air. 'Did Joel Mills kill my mother?'

A shadow passed over Miss Ross's face and she took a deep breath. 'Joel was Cassie's pack leader and when your mother told him she wanted to leave the pack he became angry. You have to understand; it *is* possible to leave a pack without issue but the reason your mother wanted to leave was what caused the tension.'

'Why did she want to leave?'

'Sebastian,' Miss Ross said softly. 'Your mother fell in love with Sebastian when they were young but he was a hunter and she came from a family of werewolves. They tried to hide their relationship from the world but Sebastian's brother found out the truth. He didn't have the hunter gene but he understood the laws.'

'So my dad threatened to expose them?' It was a guess, but understanding how cruel my father could be, I presumed that I wasn't far off the truth.

Miss Ross nodded. 'Your dad told them he would go to the pack and tell them everything unless she agreed to marry him.'

Elizabeth sucked in a deep breath. I'd moved beyond being shocked by my dad's actions long ago and urged Miss Ross to continue.

'Your mother had no choice but to agree. They got married and then went on to have Zak. She tried so hard to make a go of the marriage and forget about Sebastian, but the pull was too great. They were like magnets and every time they tried to separate, an unseen force would pull them back together.'

'That's why Dr Roberts has all the photographs of Mia's mum in his office.' Elizabeth squeezed my hand as she spoke and I was once again grateful that she was with me.

'Yes, he never stopped loving her,' Miss Ross said with true affection in her voice.

•• • ● •• •

AFTER MISS ROSS left, I squared my shoulders and leant back against my bed. I couldn't feel sorry for Sebastian; what he was doing to the werewolves wasn't right. I thought about Terry. He was a human being ninety-nine per cent of the time. Torturing him wasn't the right thing to do—it was beyond cruel.

'Do you think it's Felicity that hunts them?' Elizabeth asked as she collected the files from the bed.

'Yes, I do. She's the one with a secret key to the lab, and I heard Terry's screams when she was down there with him.'

'She isn't just catching them, is she?'

'No, she isn't, but I don't know if Sebastian is even aware that she's torturing them for pleasure.'

'Are you going to tell him?'

I flopped onto the bed and picked up the letter my mum had written to Sebastian.

'I can't tell him without owning up to our part in all of this.'

'So what now?'

I couldn't answer her. I didn't know who to trust to help us. I glanced over the letter again, my eyes settling on the final words.

'I believe in what you are doing...I hope you carry on without me.'

It was my mum's wish that Sebastian continue to work on the serum, but why? Realisation hit me and a chill spread over my skin. She did it for us. Me and Zak. I'd only just found out that it was even possible that I could turn into a werewolf, but beyond the shock and horror I hadn't given much thought to the practical side of things. Would I be prepared to undergo treatment to avoid turning?

'If my mum wanted Sebastian to finish the serum, I think she hoped it would work on Zak, and me.'

Elizabeth stopped what she was doing and sat beside me.

'But Zak's the alpha. The pack needs him.'

'I doubt he would be interested in a cure.' I felt despondent that I didn't know anything about my brother any more.

'Your mum was a willing test subject, Mia. From what Miss Ross told us, Sebastian treated her with care.'

'So she wasn't shoved in the animal cages then,' I mumbled.

Elizabeth wrapped her arm around my shoulder.

'We'll figure it all out, don't worry.'

The smile I gave her didn't quite reach my eyes. I felt numb all over. When she moved away, I wrapped my arms around my legs, hugging them to my chest like a protective barrier. I couldn't shake the feeling that it was Sebastian's fault that my mum had died.

There was a faint tap at the door and a small square envelope appeared under the gap. We both stared at it for a while until Elizabeth scooped it up and handed it to me.

Inside was a photo of my mum and Sebastian; they looked so happy, with twinkling eyes and radiant smiles. On the reverse was a short note from Miss Ross.

> *Sebastian was protecting you by not telling you the truth about your mother's death. He arranged for the police to notify you about the car accident. He wanted to finish his work before Zak came of age and turned for the first time.*

'I guess that explains why your mum wanted Zak to go to Sebastian instead of Joel.' Elizabeth said over my shoulder.

If Frank had ever realised that your mum was secretly seeing his brother, it would have been catastrophic for you and Zak. Sebastian thought he was doing the right thing by keeping the truth from you.

I gave a little huff as I read her words and thought about how catastrophic my life had been regardless of whether we had known the truth or not. I wished that my dad had chosen to cherish and care for me in the aftermath of Mum's death instead of beating me. It was as if he had taken all his hatred for Sebastian out on me.

Miss Ross's note continued, *Look closely at the photo, Mia. What similarities can you see?*

A wave of understanding washed over me as I thought about how my dad would look at me from beneath a furrowed brow. His face would twist into a mask of loathing for the little girl with dark eyes and long brown curls. As I reached my teenage years I had always been so grateful that I hadn't inherited his lacklustre mouse-brown hair but had a deeper, richer hair colour—the identical colour to Sebastian's.

At the bottom of the note, Miss Ross had scrawled a single sentence.

Yes, Mia, Sebastian is your real father.

FOURTEEN

I couldn't sleep. The room felt claustrophobic and I longed to escape to the woods beyond the academy. If I was honest, I longed to see Cody and tell him everything I'd discovered. To share my world-changing news. Sebastian was my real dad. I didn't know how to even start to handle that.

Part of me was shocked that my mum had cheated, although the overwhelming evidence proved that she had loved Sebastian above anyone else. There was also a part of me relieved to discover Frank wasn't my flesh and blood.

I'd always wondered if that violent gene was hereditary and after going all ninja on Felicity, I'd questioned it even more.

Lizzie and I had talked long into the night about it, not necessarily looking for answers but just voicing our thoughts. It had helped. Eventually, she'd fallen asleep and now here I was staring at my mum's file and wishing I could drift into a dreamless slumber.

I flipped back to the notes and resumed reading the handwritten entries. It read like a personal diary with Sebastian mentioning their conversations as he administered the injections. Stories about life, me and Zak, and how they would be reunited one day.

It felt strange to be reading something so private, even if it was about my mum.

At the bottom of the page was a hastily written addition, the messy scrawl almost illegible. I could just make out a few of the sentences.

The serum is working—Joel has found out about us—Cassie is injured. I can't believe Joel bit her, but I'm so proud that she fought back—side effects—catastrophic results—immunity to the werewolf venom has been stripped away— I can't save her—bite infection worsening—she can't self heal—I can't save her—I can't...

The final words remained unwritten, instead the ink trailed down the page as if Sebastian had lost the will to write any more.

Everything was different now. Things were going to change. I didn't know how I was going to cope with what was coming, but as I listened to the soft snores of my roommate, I knew, without any doubt, I wouldn't have to cope alone this time.

•••●•••

AFTER THE STARTLING revelation that my uncle was, in fact, my father, I managed to successfully avoid all contact with him for the next few days. I needed time and space to get my head around it all. With the end-of-term assessments, it was easy to throw myself into schoolwork and training.

Miss Ross managed to get my ban lifted, telling Sebastian how isolation would only damage my mental health further and that if I was going to heal I needed to mix with the other students. This meant I could attend regular classes, much to Elizabeth's delight, but I made sure to stay far away from Felicity.

The redhead had made a few snarky comments on my first day back, but ultimately she kept her distance. The faint outline of her bruised eye stopped me from seeking her out and confronting her about Terry. That and the fact Sebastian was still unaware of my involvement in the werewolf's escape.

I hadn't managed to sort through all my emotions yet. Discovering the truth about who my family were had been like hitting a brick wall at full speed. Finding out I was descended from werewolves and the result of an illicit relationship had blown my entire existence apart.

'Ready for the sparring assessment?' Elizabeth bounced up and down, balancing on her toes and jabbed her fists forward in quick succession. 'Our annual Karate Kid-meets-Buffy tournament to the death.'

I remembered Miss Ross telling me about the assessments during my first one-on-one session, but I didn't remember her telling me it was to the death.

At the look of absolute horror on my face, Elizabeth laughed out loud before assuring me that 'death' meant a winner's medal.

'Nope,' I mumbled, struggling into my pumps. 'The last thing I want to do is punch anyone in the face again. Look what happened last time.'

'In my humble opinion, Felicity deserved what she got, and after what Miss Ross told us, the girl needed a good slap to shut her up.'

'I guess it did give Terry a few days' break while she was recovering in the nurse's office.'

We giggled as we made our way through the gardens towards the gymnasium. Adam rushed over to give Elizabeth a good-luck kiss, and I couldn't help but roll my eyes at just how damn cute the two of them were.

SHELLEY WILSON

When the handsome groundsman had vanished back behind the rose bushes, I elbowed Elizabeth and wiggled my eyebrows.

'So, it's going well?'

She lowered her voice to a whisper and leant in close.

'It is, but we've had to take it slow the last few days because Terry was in Adam's room and it would have been, well...awkward.'

I laughed, imagining how Terry would react to playing gooseberry to two teenagers. He didn't strike me as a romantic type of werewolf.

My mind flitted to Cody. We hadn't spoken since my little outburst in the woods, and I was beginning to regret being so upset with him. He was the first person I'd wanted to tell when I found out about Sebastian. I knew he was only trying to protect his own family and, in his own weird way, he was also shielding me. I decided to send him a message to meet me at the overhang after the assessments were over and make it up to him.

My cheeks grew hot as I contemplated the various ways I could say sorry. Our first kiss still vivid in my memory, I prayed that the tournament wouldn't take long.

·· ● ··

FOUR SECTIONS WERE cordoned off inside the gymnasium, each with a fighting arena in the centre and rope barriers. Along the far wall were several rows of chairs full of everyone's family members. Elizabeth waved at a couple sitting in the back row, and I deduced that the beautiful woman who shared Elizabeth's long blonde hair and blue eyes was her mum. I spotted the imposing figure of Felicity's father sitting in the front row between Sebastian and Miss Ross, his wide shoulders held taut as he surveyed the students with a predatory glare while we streamed into the gym.

Sebastian stood and walked into the centre of the hall, turning to face the visiting guests with a forced smile on his

147

face. He had shaved and wore a clean suit, but the dark circles under his eyes were a giveaway that he was a troubled man. I felt a sharp pang of pity but shook it off. I couldn't afford to care for the man who had ultimately caused my mum's death, even if he was my biological father. If he hadn't given her the flawed serum, she would have healed and been alive today.

It was hard to believe Sebastian was unaware that I was his daughter. My mum had confided in my teacher but never dared to utter the truth for fear of what my dad would do if he found out. With the benefit of hindsight, I now realised that *Frank* wasn't stupid and had clearly worked it out for himself. Something Sebastian had failed to do.

'Ladies and gentlemen, welcome to Hood Academy.' Sebastian's voice was clear and crisp as he spoke to the assembled crowd. 'Before we begin the tournament, I have the great pleasure of swearing in our newest member of the academy, Mia Roberts.'

I flinched as all eyes in the gymnasium slid my way. My cheeks were burning as I made my way to where Sebastian was standing.

When Miss Ross told me about taking the oath, she failed to mention the pomp and ceremony involved. My hands felt slick and I surreptitiously wiped them down my T-shirt. The gymnasium fell silent and the only sound I could hear was the roar of blood pumping through my veins. My stomach churned as I drew closer to Sebastian.

He gave me a tight smile as I approached and lifted a tattered old brown leather book. Taking my hand, he placed it on top of the book and rested his hand over mine. I felt myself tense up at his touch, but he misread it for nerves.

'Don't worry, Mia. It'll be over very quickly,' he whispered.

Lifting his head, he spoke loudly so the gathered guests could hear.

'To every pack, a cub is born. The hunter shall be unleashed to protect and serve. Mia Roberts, do you swear to uphold the hunters' oath and serve this academy and cause?'

I really wanted to tell him to shove his oath and run screaming from the gymnasium, but instead I nodded my head and replied, 'I do.'

'Then I hereby declare you to be a hunter of the realm.'

There was thunderous applause from the parents and students and I wondered if I'd burn in hell if my werewolf gene were ever triggered.

Sebastian patted my shoulder to dismiss me and turned to address the audience.

'You are here today to support your children in this assessment. These tournaments have been held for many generations, and the student with the most points at the end will win the coveted prize.' He held aloft a gold medal on a red ribbon, and the crowd erupted into applause.

'So we get to beat the crap out of each other for a chunk of metal?' I whispered to Elizabeth as I returned to her side.

She snorted. 'Pretty much. It's one point for a strike to the arm, two for the legs and four for a body blow. Just let whoever you're paired with punch you in the gut a couple of times and then you'll be out and can sit back and watch.'

She had a valid argument, but deep in my stomach, I could feel the rumblings of my competitive streak. I'd never bothered to interact with anyone at my old school and I certainly wouldn't have taken part in tournaments, but joining Hood Academy, meeting Elizabeth, Cody and Miss Ross, had awoken something inside me. Something dangerous.

Sebastian had taken his seat and was talking to Felicity's father when I made my way to zone number one. We were allocated a partner and stood at the barrier until Mr Peterson, the boxing coach turned commentator, called our names.

One by one the pairs were ushered into the arena. The cries of the parents carried above the grunts and yelps of the students in the ring. A young girl called Helen stood next to me as our names were called. She was slightly smaller than me, but I'd seen her using the staff in training and knew she was fast and methodical. My inner wolf, if I even had one, was likely to slink off with its tail between its legs as soon as the whistle blew.

'Hey, Mia.' Helen grinned at me. 'I'll try not to hurt you too much.'

She said it in jest, I knew that, but I couldn't stop the roar of power that shot through my core and into my limbs on hearing her words. Helen's eyes grew wide as I growled, the sound escaping before I could stop it. I clenched my fists and waited for the whistle.

•• ● ••

I COULD HEAR Elizabeth's shouts of encouragement above the overwhelming din in the gymnasium. We had been fighting for well over an hour, and I had moved through the tournament with surprising ease. Elizabeth was out of the contest and sporting a fat lip courtesy of a large girl called Nessie. Helen sat by her side clutching a cold compress to her bruised shoulder caused by my roundhouse kick.

It had surprised us both when I launched my full-scale attack. I wasn't sure how or when I had retained all my training skills but I was able to use them with deadly precision. I wondered if Sebastian was proud of me.

'Mia Roberts and Stacy Calver, please move to zone four.' Mr Peterson's voice boomed out over the hubbub. He was in charge of the scoreboard and directing the students to their respective pairings and appeared to be enjoying the brutality far too much.

Something that felt oddly like pride washed over me as I approached the next contest, and I felt my shoulders straighten and my chin lift. Never had I felt this powerful or so in control. I'd had any semblance of confidence thrashed out of me from an early age and I honestly thought that capability was gone for good.

I understood all too well the irony of it being Sebastian who I had to thank for bringing me to Hood Academy and for persuading me to give the school a chance. I risked a glance in his direction and caught him watching me. A warm smile lit up his face as I took my place on the mat opposite my next opponent.

Felicity's father was concentrating his attention on the other side of the hall where his daughter was pulverising her latest victim. I felt the side of my mouth twitch slightly as I gave Sebastian the smallest of smiles. The look of delight that flashed across his face touched a long dormant part of my heart. I tried to shake it off. I didn't want to let him in. I couldn't form any attachment to the man other than that of a distant relative. So why was I so happy to have his support on the sidelines? And why did it feel so right to have him there supporting me?

The whistle blew, bringing me back to the present with a jolt. Stacy secured her first point as she took advantage of my distracted mind. I rolled my shoulders back and bounced from one foot to the other then circled my prey. It was at that moment I realised that *prey* is exactly what she was. If I did become a werewolf, I would need to hunt and this tournament was becoming a useful experiment for honing my skills.

Stacy didn't see me coming as I leapt forward and punched her once in the stomach and then swung my leg out to swipe her feet from under her. She fell to the ground with a thud and the referee waved his flag in my direction.

'Six points to Mia Roberts,' he shouted.

Elizabeth cheered and I saw Sebastian rise to his feet, clapping his hands enthusiastically.

I bowed once more to Stacy, who glared at me from across the mat. Too bad. My competitive streak was strong, and I was going to take her down.

•• • ● • ••

IT WAS LATE afternoon when I finally got a break. Although each fight didn't take very long, I was still exhausted when Elizabeth pulled me out into the fresh air of the gardens. Adam was waiting with a long, cold drink and I took it from him gratefully.

'You are rocking this tournament,' Elizabeth squealed. 'I'm so damn proud of you.'

I grinned at her as I handed the empty glass back to Adam.

'It's like all the training has suddenly clicked and I can anticipate everyone's moves. I don't think Stacy will ever speak to me again, though.'

'Pft, no great loss.' Elizabeth flicked her hand to the side as if to dismiss Stacy's entire existence. 'You're a way better fighter than her anyway.'

'How many fights do you have left?' Adam asked.

'Two. I'm through to the semi-finals.'

'That's amazing, Mia,' he said, lowering his voice and adding, 'must be that werewolf DNA.'

I thumped him on the arm and Elizabeth clipped him round the ear at the same time as he burst out laughing.

'We don't know that Mia will inherit that gene,' she scolded him. 'She could just be an extremely skilled hunter.'

'Yeah, so you better watch it, Adam, or I'll kick your butt too.'

We laughed together, chatting and discussing tactics for the next half an hour, enjoying the relative peace of the gardens. Once they cleared the space and erected one big fighting arena in the centre of the room then the remaining competitors could return to the gymnasium.

The air was much colder as the afternoon vanished and the sky darkened. I found my gaze wandering to the treeline, and I thought about Cody and the wolves.

'I wonder if Terry got home okay.'

'He did,' Adam said. 'I saw him earlier today in Ravens-hood. He was in Taylor's Coffee Shop with his brothers.'

I snapped my head around and gawped at Adam.

'You saw them all?'

Adam nodded.

'Was Zak there?'

'I don't know what he looks like, Mia, but there were three others with Terry, so I can only assume one of them was Zak.'

I hadn't seen my brother in nearly ten years. I clung onto the faint memory of his dark hair and hazel-coloured eyes, the developing muscles, and the early signs of stubble on his face. He was sixteen back then, still so young and naïve. He would be twenty-five now and was a pack leader. I was sure the muscles would be well defined and he might even have a full beard.

My chest felt constricted and I struggled to breathe. I was crazy mad at him but also missed him so much. Once this tournament was over, I would ask Cody to set up a meeting. It was time to be reunited with my brother.

Mr Peterson's booming voice cut through my musings as he announced the first semi-final match.

Elizabeth jumped to her feet and held out her hand to help me up.

'Come on, champ. It's time to win that medal.'

•• ● ●••

IF I BELIEVED in fate, or planets aligning, today would have been the perfect day to confirm those theories. As I walked into the gym sandwiched between Elizabeth and Adam, I looked up to see my name scrawled across the whiteboard directly above Felicity Parker's name.

The air left my lungs instantly and I stopped dead in my tracks causing Elizabeth to stumble as she spun towards my now motionless body.

'What is it?'

'I'm paired with Felicity,' I said.

Elizabeth looked over at the board and then closed the distance between us, grasping my hands tightly in hers.

'You can do this, Mia. You have pretty much cleared the board of other competitors. She's just another student who stands in the way of you winning that medal.'

I nodded blankly at my friend. I wanted to tell her that I wasn't scared or worried. I was elated. The gods, goddesses or universal energy had delivered this to me and I wasn't about to mess it up.

I looked into the bright blue eyes of my best friend and squeezed her hands.

'Don't worry about me, Lizzie. I'm going to kick that bitch's ass.'

•• • ● • ••

WE WERE THE second team to fight, having already watched one of Felicity's squad, Elena Fields, obliterate Nicole Berry to secure her place in the final. Elena stalked up and down the gym like a lioness on the hunt, eyeing us both with hungry eyes.

It annoyed me and I prayed once more that I was the one who made it through this fight and got to wipe the smug smile off her face. Although I had the strangely comforting thought that if Felicity did beat me, she wouldn't think twice about taking down her friend.

I took up my position opposite the redhead, who glared at me from across the mat. She was clearly unimpressed that I'd made it this far in the tournament.

Mr Peterson drew us close and repeated the rules of the fight. We nodded our understanding and stepped away far enough to bow, first to the referee and then to each other.

The whistle blew and we began the fluid dance of sizing each other up and looking for an opening. My heart was hammering in my chest as adrenalin surged through me, powering my confidence and keeping my mind sharp.

I watched her step to the right and then to the left, her long legs carrying her across the mat with grace. My fingers ached from clenching my hands into tight fists, but I remained in a defensive stance. We mirrored one another as we explored every inch of the mat, both of us weaving and ducking, neither ready to strike first.

Felicity jabbed forward. I sidestepped her, blocking her strike and managing to get in an uppercut to the gut.

'Four points to Mia Roberts!'

Half of the audience cheered, the other half gasped.

I stepped away and looked over at the front row. Felicity's father's face was a mask of stone. He stared at his daughter with a loathing that I understood all too well.

I darted forward and landed a punch on her left shoulder. She yelped and circled towards me, baring her teeth like a rabid dog. She jumped and spun in a full circle, knocking me off my feet with a roundhouse kick. I flew into the referee who managed to stay upright and keep me from hitting the gymnasium floor.

I steadied myself and nodded my appreciation to the referee, walking back into the arena with purposeful strides. I caught Elizabeth's eye as she gave me a double thumbs up sign. Sebastian had moved away from Felicity's father and was now sitting next to Elizabeth and Miss Ross. They looked like a rent-a-crowd and it made me smile.

'Something funny?' Felicity spat the words at me.

'Not at all, I just hope they've kept your bed warm in the nurse's office.'

Felicity roared and sprang at me, her anger wiping away all rational thought and training. I punched out in quick succession, left then right, two blows to the chest.

'Eight points to Mia Roberts!'

Felicity screamed and swung her fist forward, aiming for my head. I lifted my right arm to block her advance, pushing her away and slamming my own fist into her nose. I heard the crunch as I circled away from her.

The referee blew his whistle and called me over.

'No direct blows to the head, Miss Roberts. Two points will be deducted.'

I didn't care. This fight wasn't about the points any more. I was doing this for Terry, for Cody and my brother. For all the wolves that Felicity and her family had tortured over the years. I was going to win for my mum, for Elizabeth and Miss Ross, for Adam and all the students that ever feared the bully who stood in front of me.

SHELLEY WILSON

FIFTEEN

I nestled the gold medal into the folds of my jumper, feeling the heavy weight of it against my chest. I never wanted to take it off again. I'd beaten Felicity by two points and went on to annihilate Elena by eight points to claim the prize.

Felicity's father had stormed out of the gymnasium before the end of his daughter's fight, and I spotted Sebastian hurry out after him. I'm sure it hadn't helped his cause that his 'niece' had beaten the main benefactor's only daughter.

I didn't have time to think about that now. Darkness blanketed the sky, and I was eager to get to the overhang and speak to Cody. Winning the medal had pushed all my angst and disappointments to the side. I wanted to share my happy news and, somewhere inside me, I hoped that Zak would hear about my win and be proud of his sister. After seeing Felicity's father at the tournament today, I understood just how dangerous it was for Zak to come anywhere near the academy. I needed to look beyond my own needs and appreciate that being pack leader had its risks. He knew where I was, and I would be waiting when it was safe for us to meet.

I left the building and walked through the garden towards the patio doors of Adam's room. I wanted to tell Elizabeth that I was sneaking out again.

The gravel crunched underfoot as I manoeuvred my way along the path. When I reached the centre of the garden, I heard the low murmuring of voices.

Through the curtain of leaves, I could see two figures sitting on the old stone bench, beneath the willow tree. The pale light of the bulbous moon glistened off Elizabeth's long hair. She threw her head back and laughed. The sheer delight at making her happy was evident on Adam's face. It filled my heart with a warmth that I'd thought was alien to me. Over the past few weeks, Elizabeth had become an important part of my life, like the sister I never had.

Her happiness meant a lot and I knew that Adam would continue to make her laugh that loud for a long time. Her beautiful face lit up when she smiled at him, and I was genuinely happy for her.

I let the branches fall back to shield them from my view as Adam leant in and tenderly kissed Elizabeth. They didn't need an audience.

The warmth I felt at my friends' happiness spread through my limbs as I thought about my own private rendezvous. Quickening my pace, I wound through the thicket of trees, eager to see Cody and tell him about winning the tournament.

As I reached the edge of the academy wall, I surveyed the empty windows of the house. All clear.

I raced across the lawn at full speed, but before I could reach the shelter of the animal cages, a single figure stepped out from behind the wall and blocked my path.

I skidded to a halt in front of Felicity, conscious that I was in full view of the academy windows. If anyone spotted me out of the building, I was in deep trouble.

Shit.

'Going somewhere?'

Her squad stepped out to stand behind her. Elena grinned insanely, folding her arms across her chest. Goon number two followed suit. They looked like a couple of bizarre statues.

I couldn't afford for Sebastian to see me near the forest, not after he had forbidden me to venture into the woods at night, so I edged to my right in a bid to shelter behind the bushes. As if expecting my move, Felicity mirrored my steps, forcing me onto the open lawn.

'I don't have time for your pathetic games, Felicity.'

Like a penalty shooter, I had three options: go left, go right or straight down the middle. I chose the last option and was pleased to see the shock register fleetingly on Felicity's face as I barrelled into her.

I shoved her hard as I passed, using the full force of my body. She regained her composure quickly and snapped her fingers. The two goons sprang to life and grabbed my arms in a vice-like grip. I flinched and tried to pull myself free, but they were surprisingly strong.

'Not this time, Roberts.' Felicity's face twisted into a snarl as she skulked forward, bringing her nose close to mine. 'You humiliated me today and I'm going to show you what happens to people who get on my bad side. Your uncle can't save you this time.'

I launched my head forward in a short, sharp snap and felt the crunch as her nose burst open. Blood spurted over her face, dripping off her chin, as she staggered back with a scream.

She swung her fist and connected with my left cheek. I felt my lip split and licked the blood away quickly. She could keep punching me all night, but I refused to show her any weakness.

I braced myself for the next onslaught but it never came. Instead, the girls dragged me down the path behind the animal cages, wrestling my phone out of my jacket pocket as they pushed and shoved me down the path. My first thought was that we were heading to the overhang and I hoped that Cody would be there to help me, but they veered left and worked their way down the path leading straight to the cages.

One of the iron doors stood ajar. I didn't register their intent until they shoved me unceremoniously through the opening. I landed heavily on the concrete floor, my hands and knees taking the brunt of the fall. The cage smelt of wet dogs. As I sat back on my legs, the cage door slammed shut behind me.

I swung around in time to see Felicity click the padlock through the door, locking me in.

'What the hell, Felicity?' Fuming, I stood and grasped the bars of the cage, pushing my face up close to the metal. 'Let me out.'

She pressed her sleeve against her face, trying to stem the flow of blood from her busted nose.

'You're not going anywhere, wolf girl.'

'What did you call me?' I could feel the anger stirring deep in my gut.

'Wolf girl! Don't pretend you're clueless. You must have worked it all out by now. Your precious mother was a wolf and it drove Sebastian to near madness. Now the academy is at risk again, and it's all because of you.'

She stabbed a finger through the bars and I used all my strength to avoid biting it.

'My mum was a good person and she wanted to leave her pack to live a human life,' I said quietly. 'When I get out of here, I'm going to do the same.'

Felicity laughed hysterically. With her face covered in blood, she looked deranged, almost demonic.

'The pack protect their own, so if it's proof you need that you inherited your mother's genes then allow me to educate you.' She moved to the side and Elena stepped closer, holding a small crossbow in one hand.

I didn't have time to move or cry out as she fired it through the bars, the bolt hitting me hard in my left shoulder. The agony was immediate; a hot, searing scream of pain shot through me as the force of the bolt sent me crashing into the far wall.

I slid to the floor, tears coursing down my face as I grabbed the shaft and tried to tug it free. Blood poured down my arms and chest.

Felicity stood close to the locked door and sneered down at me.

'The pack protect their own; you'll see it soon enough, wolf girl.'

The three of them walked away as if they'd been on a calm stroll through the grounds.

I swore as I tugged again at the bolt; it was in deep and every movement caused more blood loss.

Shit.

The animal cage was empty aside from an old tin bucket with a hole in the bottom. Dragging myself across the filthy floor, I grasped the handle. Swinging it hard, I smashed it against the iron bars. The vibration shot through my limbs and made my teeth hurt, but the loud clang echoed out into the woods with a satisfying sound.

Someone would hear. Someone would come.

I lifted the bucket again and swung it repeatedly until my arm grew tired.

·· • ● • ··

THERE WAS A definite chill in the air, or perhaps my limbs were numb from the loss of blood. Either way, I was freezing. Felicity hadn't returned and so far my lame attempts to call for help had remained unanswered. Part of me hoped that Elizabeth and Adam would take a romantic amble through the woods and find my crumpled form, but no such luck.

The bolt from the crossbow, still embedded in my shoulder, hurt like hell. I'd ripped a strip of fabric from the bottom of my T-shirt and tried to bind the wound as best I could to stem the flow of blood.

I felt light-headed. I was cold to my bones. I was alone.

As if in answer to my prayers, I heard a rustle in the distant forest: the unmistakable crunch of boots on the ground.

'Help!' My voice cracked slightly and I coughed to try to loosen up my vocal chords before trying again. 'Please, help me!'

Like a vision sent by the angels, Cody stepped out of the treeline and stopped short. His obvious shock at seeing me locked in a cage and covered in blood subsided fairly quickly, and he cleared the space between us in a couple of strides.

'What the hell happened?'

'Long story,' I said, threading my arm through the bars so I could hold his hand.

'You're like ice, Mia.'

He examined the bolt and wound in my shoulder with a grim set to his jaw.

'Who did this to you?'

'There's a girl with an inherent hatred of wolves, and as my mother was one, she's taken it upon herself to make my life a living hell.'

I shuffled towards the door, and it took all my strength to pull myself up to standing. I grabbed the padlock and wiggled it.

'Have you got a penknife or anything that will break the lock open?'

Cody felt in his pockets and then began searching the compressed soil outside the animal cages looking for any kind of tool that would suffice. There was nothing and I felt the wave of Cody's anger and fear hit me as he raised his eyes to mine.

'I need to go get help,' he said, taking a step backwards.

'No! Please, Cody, don't leave me.'

'I *have* to, Mia. You've lost so much blood and you need medical help. I'll go get my brothers. They'll know what to do.'

I flinched away from the cage door as he stepped forward and took hold of my hands through the bars. As situations went, this one sucked, but I didn't want to sit in the dark on my own for a moment longer.

'I'll fetch Zak.'

'No! It's dangerous for him to come here. If Sebastian sees Zak, he'll try to capture him and inject that horrible serum into him.'

'Sebastian won't find out. I'll run fast and be back before you know it. Zak's your brother, Mia. He'll want to help.'

I felt a rush of heat flood through my system and even though I knew it came from Cody and his wolf genes, I couldn't help but associate the warmth with the prospect of seeing my brother again.

'I'll be fast. Tomorrow is a full moon so my senses and reactions are already heightened.'

He leant close to the bars and pulled me gently forward, kissing me lightly on my split and bloody lips.

'I'll be back soon,' he whispered.

Cody shrugged out of his jacket and passed it through the cage bars, helping me slip it around my shoulders. His scent wrapped itself around me and calmed my frayed nerves.

'I'll see you soon.' I said it more to convince myself than as a goodbye.

He nodded and turned towards the treeline, releasing my hand only an inch at a time as if it hurt him as much as it pained me to lose that physical contact.

I watched him walk away across the dirt track heading to the bushes and waited for him to turn around one last time. I knew he would because it was the kind of thing I'd do. We were more alike than either of us would let on.

As his shoulders shifted in my direction, there was a blur of movement followed by a feral cry. I shouted out in warning but it was too late. Felicity pushed through the branches and swung her staff at Cody, beating him square on the back and knocking him off his feet.

OATH BREAKER

Felicity and her two goons towered over Cody, hitting him repeatedly with their staffs. The sound of wood on flesh filled the air and a wave of nausea rushed over me.

'Cody!' I screamed his name and rattled at the cage door, desperate to get to him.

Felicity moved away from her friends and smirked at me. The silvery light cast from the moon high up in the sky highlighted the evil glint in her eyes.

'Wolf for a mother and wolf for a boyfriend. I shouldn't have expected anything less.'

'Leave him alone, Felicity. It's me you've got the issue with, not him.'

She laughed, a high-pitched hysterical laugh that stopped her goons in their tracks. The three of them circled towards me. I glanced over their shoulder to where Cody lay still on the ground. Elena prodded her stick through the bars, taunting me.

'My mother was murdered by a wolf,' Felicity said, her voice dripping with venom. 'I watched it happen right in front of me.'

'Yeah, well, both my parents were murdered by wolves and yet I've learned to forgive.'

'Forgive scum like that?' She pointed her staff in Cody's direction. His shoulders were hunched over, but he was trying to push himself up. I looked back at Felicity, eager to keep her eyes on me and not on Cody.

'They deserve to die,' she shouted through the iron bars at me.

I needed to stall and give Cody time to recover. He could still get away and fetch help.

'Where would you be if there were no werewolves, Felicity?' I stepped backwards and held my hands out palms facing upwards, the action causing pain to flare through my shoulder. I winced but continued, 'You'd be out of a job, attending a normal school where the popular kids would kick your ass. You'd be a nobody.'

Felicity's cheek twitched in the moonlight and I knew I'd struck a nerve. I pushed a little more, digging at her with my words, hoping for a reaction. It was a trick I'd picked up from my father.

'Of course, you already know what it's like to be a nobody, don't you? I bet *Daddy* thinks you're a waste of space after losing the tournament to a *wolf girl.*'

The taunting worked and Felicity launched herself at the cage, flinging her arms through the bars in an attempt to scratch my eyes out. I grabbed her wrists and bent them backwards so she couldn't back up and get away. She screamed and kicked out at the bars.

The pain in my shoulder was almost too much to bear, but I couldn't lose my advantage over the redhead.

'Open the gate and I'll let her go,' I shouted at Elena who stood open-mouthed watching events unfold.

She fumbled for the key to the padlock and rushed to the door. Her hands were shaking so much that she dropped the key twice until I finally heard the clunk of the lock.

'Throw the padlock into the woods, open the door and then step back, both of you.'

Elena and minion number two did as I asked, moving away from where I held Felicity, who was still spitting and swearing at me.

When they were far enough away, I released Felicity's hands and made a run for the open doorway. Stepping out into the clearing, I took in a lungful of the forest air, a welcome relief after the wet-dog smell mingled with my blood.

Felicity threw herself at me, grabbing the bolt in my shoulder and twisting. I screamed and fell to my knees, taking her down with me.

'I'm going to kill you,' she cried.

At that moment, when I looked into her eyes, I believed that she would indeed kill me. I'd seen loathing, hatred and wickedness in my father's eyes on numerous occasions, so I recognised it when I saw it. Felicity wasn't just a nasty school bully, she was evil incarnate, and if I was going to get out of this situation alive, I would have to fight dirty.

I grabbed a handful of her long red hair, and using my good arm I swung my fist up, connecting with the underside of Felicity's chin. Her head snapped backwards, giving me the space I needed to wriggle out from under her.

Leaping to my feet, I moved out of her reach. With the woods behind me, I faced the animal cages and could just make out the twinkling lights from the academy in the distance. I momentarily wished that Sebastian would come looking for me, but then I remembered Cody and thought better of it.

As if reading my mind, Felicity grabbed her staff from the floor and sprinted across the clearing to where Cody was crouched, rocking on his hands and knees.

She swung the stick and I heard the sickening crack as it collided with his head. He pitched onto his side and started twitching and shaking all over. Felicity held the staff above her head. She was ready to continue with her barrage of abuse but stopped in mid-swing to observe Cody's strange movements.

I wanted to run to his side but something inside me warned against it.

The convulsing grew in intensity, and he looked like he had lost all control of his body. A ripping sound filled the air at the same time as a low, deep growl rumbled from the back of Cody's throat.

I was transfixed as I watched Cody's clothing shred and fall to the ground. He cried out in pain but I willed my feet to stay put. There was nothing I could do to help him now. His hands stretched out in my direction as if he was reaching for me, but where his fingernails should have been, long claws broke through the skin. He arched his back and I watched the smooth, pallid skin disappear as his spine contorted and snapped into an alternative shape. His nakedness faded under a shiny coat of golden fur. His beautiful face distorted as a long snout and fangs tore through the flesh.

The wolf snarled and flicked a long pink tongue over its teeth, sniffing the air as it uncurled to its full height. It cast its gaze across the clearing, looking at each of us in turn. I gasped as it looked at me. Its eyes hadn't changed. They told me that Cody was still inside, and my heart played tug of war between fear and friendship. Felicity cowered beneath it as it grew to the size of a horse, but I saw the shift in her stance as her hunter instincts kicked in and she swung the staff at the werewolf. At Cody.

In one fluid movement, the wolf pounced, its jaw wide open and the sharp fangs sparkling in the moonlight. Felicity collided with Cody and then screamed as he bit down on her shoulder, causing the staff to fall harmlessly out of reach. He didn't let go and shook her like a rag doll. Blood sprayed across the clearing hitting my face. Elena yelled and grabbing her friend's arm, they tried to make a run for the woods, but as I watched them abandon their leader to her fate, a row of eyes in the treeline halted their progress.

I stood frozen to the spot as six huge wolves stalked out of the trees. The biggest was a dark brown wolf with massive paws and hazel eyes. It stopped and raised its head towards me, sniffing the air. I felt a trickle of fear along my spine as I remembered the last time I'd looked into those eyes. It was just after the creature tore my dad's throat out. This fearsome beast that stood in front of me was the wolf that had saved my life. Suddenly all the pieces fell into place.

'Zak?' I whispered.

SIXTEEN

Elena and her companion were hysterical and remained huddled together as they backed away from the advancing wolves. I wondered if Miss Ross would reprimand them for crumbling under pressure.

Zak padded forward and stood over Cody. The difference in their size shocked me. I had thought that human Cody was tall but seeing his wolf form beside the towering form of an alpha put the whole leader-of-the pack vibe into perspective. His dark brown fur shimmered in the moonlight, and I could make out the lines of the muscles on his limbs. His paws were as big as dinner plates and thumped the ground with a resounding echo that vibrated through our bones.

He growled and his long snout crumpled up to reveal the deadliest fangs I'd ever seen. A low, deep rumble came from his throat, and Cody bobbed his golden head up and down, dumping a bleeding Felicity on the ground.

She scrambled away from the wolves, blood pouring from her shoulder. Elena helped the redhead regain her footing as she reached the stone wall. Felicity took a shuddering breath and vomited over her friend's shoes, tears shining in her wide eyes. Their faces turned towards the wolves in terror, but I found myself in a state of fascination rather than fear. Surrounded by wolves, I faced the three girls.

'You better leave, Felicity, before anyone else gets hurt.'

'Oh, someone is going to get hurt when my father hears about this.'

There was no doubt in my mind that her father would indeed hunt Zak and his pack for harming his daughter, but that was a worry to assess at a later time. Right now, my main aim was to get rid of the girls before they provoked the wolves into another attack.

A rustling to the left of the wall echoed through the clearing and a group of shadowy shapes emerged out of the darkness. I noticed Miss Ross immediately as she planted her feet in a defensive stance and appraised the sight in front of her. Elizabeth, Adam and a couple of students I recognised stepped into the clearing, armed with staffs and crossbows, and on seeing the blood and disarray around them they all assumed a defensive position ready for a fight.

I crept forward, not wanting to startle the wolves, and held out my good arm, suspending my hand in a lame attempt to stop Miss Ross and the pupils from advancing. Zak and Cody backed away until the wolves were on the edge of the treeline and I stood between them and my fellow students.

'Please, Felicity needs a doctor. Just get her out of here.' I hoped that by showing compassion for the redhead I would be able to give the wolves some time to retreat.

Miss Ross nodded at a couple of students on her left who broke away to escort Felicity and her friends away from the clearing. Felicity's high-pitched voice carried through the night sky as she swore and berated Miss Ross's methods, asking her chaperon why they hadn't run in and killed the wolves on sight.

'Step aside, Mia.' Miss Ross's voice was calm and steady but her eyes told a different story. 'They attacked a student and need to be dealt with.'

'No! They were defending themselves. It was Felicity who attacked them. She locked me in the cages and used me as bait. They were just trying to protect me.'

As my teacher digested this new information, Sebastian burst through the bushes brandishing a shotgun. The wolves growled as one and the sound caused the hairs on the back of my neck to stand on end. Zak took a step forward and snarled, lowering his head and immense shoulders as if in readiness to pounce.

'Stop it!' I shouted. Sebastian halted in his tracks as his gaze fell upon the circle of wolves.

I turned to look at Zak. He lifted his ginormous head and blocked out the moon in the sky.

'Please, they're my friends,' I whispered.

He nodded his huge head and let out a low rumble. One by one the wolves disappeared into the trees. Cody lingered until last and only left when Zak huffed at him to move.

I heard the intake of breath from Elizabeth, Adam and Sebastian as they sucked air into their lungs, relieved to have evaded a brutal battle.

With the wolves safely out of the area and Felicity on her way to the hospital wing, I was able to assess what had just happened. It hit me like a steam train and I dropped to my knees feeling drained.

Elizabeth rushed to my side and yelped when she spotted the crossbow bolt sticking out of my shoulder. Cody's jacket had hidden it from view, but now that I had time to think about it, I started to feel a little light-headed and nauseous. Yes, I was definitely going to vomit. I bent over and coughed my guts up onto the dirt floor.

'I don't feel so good,' I said to Elizabeth as the darkness began to push at the corners of my mind. In the blurriness, I saw figures approaching me and felt Adam's strong arms under my legs and shoulders. I felt weightless as I drifted off into a deep sleep.

·· • ● • ··

THE STRONG SCENT of antiseptic roused me from a silent, dreamless sleep, and I rubbed at my nose to try to clear the smell. My eyes fluttered open but the lights were so bright it took me a while to focus.

I glanced around the sterile room of the hospital wing, remembering the events that had landed me here. Instinct made me reach for the bolt in my shoulder but it was gone. I was strapped up tightly and dressed in a highly unattractive blue jumpsuit.

'Good morning, Miss Roberts.' A wrinkly-faced doctor walked through the open doorway and grabbed my wrist. He pressed ice-cold fingers to my pulse point and monitored the second hand on his wristwatch. 'You are very lucky to be alive, my dear. You lost a lot of blood.'

I huffed, not quite sure I wanted to commit to any conversation at this early stage in our acquaintance.

'If you're up to it, I have a couple of visitors for you.'

I looked over his shoulder and spotted Elizabeth and Adam waiting in the corridor. I couldn't stop a wide grin and Dr Wrinkly took that as an invitation. He waved my friends into the room and scribbled something on a chart attached to the end of my bed before leaving us alone.

We waited until he had gone before speaking and then we all rushed to say something at once.

'Are you okay?'

'Does it hurt?'

'Thanks for everything.'

We laughed and I let my shoulders relax against the starched hospital pillow.

'I'm so glad you guys are okay.'

Elizabeth sat on the end of my bed and started fiddling with the hem of a blanket.

'What's going on, Lizzie?'

I looked across the bed at Adam who also kept his head lowered.

'Adam?'

'Felicity has been running her mouth off about you and Cody,' he said. 'Although Sebastian has tried to cover up any link.' He stood up and began pacing around the room. 'He's told everyone that you were seduced by Cody so that the wolves could try and learn the academy's secrets.'

I gawped at him.

'Your uncle has told the governors and the students that the wolves weren't able to get the information from you because you were actually working with him to capture another wolf for experimentation.'

'Oh my God, and people believe him?' I was horrified.

'Yes, the governors have no reason to doubt him, and the students believe pretty much anything they're told.'

'Everyone's going to think I'm either a failed werewolf hunter or a traitor for breaking the school's oath.'

'Sebastian was only doing what he thought was right,' Adam said. 'He's really messed up about the whole thing and has hardly left your side since we brought you in here last night.'

A flicker of warmth stirred in the pit of my stomach at Adam's words. Sebastian cared and it felt strangely comforting.

'He'll be coming to see you soon but don't let on that we told you.'

'I'll try not to,' I said, wondering if I could honestly refrain from shouting at him when he did arrive.

• • ● • •

I DIDN'T REALISE that I'd drifted off to sleep until I heard the faint sound of a chair leg scraping across the floor. I opened my eyes and saw Sebastian heading for the door.

'You don't have to go,' I whispered.

He whirled around at the sound of my voice. His face was unshaven and he wore jeans and a jumper instead of his usual smart suit, collar and tie.

'Oh, Mia, are you okay?'

I wriggled up to a sitting position and let him take hold of my hand.

'I'm fine, just a bit groggy and sore.'

'If anything happened to you I would never be able to forgive myself.'

I stopped myself from saying anything too harsh by biting my bottom lip. Instead, I offered a weak smile.

'You mean the world to me, Mia.'

I examined his face, noting the dark smudges beneath his eyes. It looked like he hadn't slept in days. Gone was the strong, confident man who had walked into my life only a few weeks ago.

'When did you last have a good meal and sleep through the night?' I asked him, surprising myself with the intensity of emotion that welled up inside me.

'It's been a testing time for the academy lately but it'll all work out for the best.'

'Best for who? You or the academy?'

He huffed and squeezed my fingers between his hands.

'You are so much like your mother, Mia. She was so full of compassion and hope for a better future, but not everyone thinks the same way.'

'If you're talking about Felicity's father, I understand that. His little princess made it quite clear why he has invested in the school. He wants to kill all the wolves—no exceptions.'

Sebastian lowered his head until it was resting on my fingers. I had the strangest urge to stroke the top of his head with my free hand.

'I can't...escape his hold,' he mumbled.

I wasn't sure what he was talking about and was about to suggest that he explain himself when he suddenly broke down. Tears soaked the bed linen as his shoulders shook with the release. I was stunned into silence. I'd never seen an adult cry. My dad hadn't even shed a tear at my mum's funeral.

'It was my fault, Mia. She'd still be alive if I'd waited until the serum was ready.'

He was babbling but I could make out every word and they chilled me to the bone.

'When your mother was injured, I sat by her bedside, just like I'm here with you now, and I willed her to get better, but she didn't. She got worse every day. The serum had taken away all her healing abilities and there was nothing I could do to help her.'

I knew that the reason my mother died was because she couldn't fight off the venom from Joel's bite. I'd read that much in her file. But why was he spilling this to me now?

He let out another wracking sob and carried on talking. 'When she passed away, I needed to cover it up, to save the academy and my work. Felicity's father said he could help. He had connections with the police commissioner. He helped me hide the truth.'

I clenched my free hand into a tight fist. That's how Felicity had known so much about me and my family when I first arrived at Hood Academy. Her dad had been blackmailing Sebastian for nearly ten years.

'Do they know that you're my real dad?'

Sebastian gave a small hiccup and lifted his head. His eyes were awash with unshed tears. His mouth dropped open as he struggled to find the words which eluded him. It told me everything I needed to know. He hadn't expected me to say that.

'No... It can't be true.'

'I'm afraid it is. Mum confided in Miss Ross and she was the one who told me. She thought I had a right to know.'

SHELLEY WILSON

'I...I half suspected at the time, but Cassie was trying to make it work with Frank, so I told myself that you must be my brother's child.'

'Well, I'm not. I'm your daughter.'

He released my fingers and ran his hands through his hair.

'What do we do now?' It only dawned on me in that moment that Sebastian might not want a daughter. Running the school and keeping his distance from the teenage element might be his only ambitions. He might not want to be a father to me, and I didn't think I could cope with anyone else rejecting me.

He stood up and walked around the room, rubbing a hand over the stubble on his chin.

'We need to find out which DNA is the most prominent.'

I blinked. Not what I was expecting to hear from my new dad.

'With any luck you'll have inherited my hunter DNA, but I don't want you to worry, Mia. If you do have your mum's genes, we can fix that.'

I watched him pace back and forth as I chewed over his words. A bubbling of dread began to inch its way up my spine as I understood his intentions.

'You're not going to do any experiments on me, Sebastian.' I folded my arms across my chest and fixed him with my sternest glare.

'I can help you,' he said, returning to sit beside me and take my hand.

'You're not listening. I don't *want* your help, I'm perfectly happy as I am.'

'Your mother would have wanted this.' He continued talking as if I hadn't said anything. 'She hoped that I could cure Zak of his lycanthropy prior to him turning for the first time, but I was too late. Joel Mills got to him first and he was lost to us.'

'Zak isn't lost,' I said quietly. 'He's the pack leader.'

'I had hoped that the pack would scatter after Mills was killed. It would have been so easy to cure the entire group, but I hadn't expected them to rally round Zak and assign him as the alpha so quickly. He was so young.'

I was still reeling from his statement about the death of Cody's parents.

'Did you have something to do with Joel's death?'

Sebastian fell silent. The darkness in his eyes told me everything I needed to know, but I wanted to hear the words. I wanted my *dad* to admit what he was.

'He killed your mother,' Sebastian said in a brisk, matter-of-fact tone. 'Or at least his venom did.'

I flung the covers off my legs and swung them over the side of the bed. Jumping to the floor, I began to back away from Sebastian.

'Did you kill them?' I asked him again.

The silence stretched out between us until eventually he answered. 'Yes, I killed them.'

My hands began shaking as I balled them into fists at my sides. My head ached from the pressure of hearing all of Sebastian's revelations.

He knocked the chair to the floor with a swipe of his hand and made me jump.

'Joel Mills was a ruthless man who made your mother's life a living hell. He denied us the future we deserved, Mia. We could have been a proper family.'

I couldn't deny that the idea of a happy home with loving parents appealed, but killing people to get them out of the picture wasn't the way to achieve it.

'Cody thought his parents were killed in a car accident. You pulled the same trick with the Mills family as you did when Mum died. Did Felicity's father cover that one up as well?'

Sebastian remained quiet.

Anger roared through my veins, and I wanted more than anything to escape this hospital room and Sebastian's company, but he was standing between me and the door.

'I want you to leave,' I said.

He dropped his gaze to the floor and I watched his shoulders slump.

'I'm sorry, Mia. Please understand that everything I do is executed with the right intentions.'

'Everything you've *done*, you mean.' I had an uneasy feeling in my gut.

He looked up at me then, but there was no emotion in his eyes. Before I could question his words he had backed out of the door. He closed it behind him and I heard the definitive click of the key in the lock.

'No!' I ran to the door and tried the handle. Locked. He had actually locked me in the hospital room.

Shit.

I frantically looked around for a window but the room didn't have one. There was only one explanation for the lack of a window—the hospital wing was in the basement of the academy and probably very close to Sebastian's laboratory. I'd survived the cruelty and horrors of living with a physically abusive father, and now I was going to die by the hand of my biological and utterly psychotic father.

Panic set in and I slid to the floor with a strangled cry. I let the tears fall as I lowered my head to my knees and wept.

SEVENTEEN

'Where am I?'

'What does Sebastian plan to do with me?'

'I want to see Elizabeth.'

Each plea landed on deaf ears as Dr Wrinkly checked my pulse, changed my bandages and gave me painkillers. I examined every tube and tablet he put in front of me for mysterious serums but the doctor was merely there to ensure I was still recovering.

Sebastian clearly needed me in optimum health to administer his crazy DNA test. I tried not to think about the results, but I was a little bit curious. Was I destined to be a wolf? My mum had only hated it because she fell in love with a hunter. Although I wouldn't call it love, I had certainly developed feelings for a wolf. Was I so similar to my mother that we could both destroy our lives because of our emotions?

I pushed the mashed potato and peas that Dr Wrinkly had delivered on his last visit around the plate. My appetite had vanished the minute Sebastian locked me in. Judging by the contents of my plate, it was early evening. The moon had been full last night and I wondered if the wolves had stayed safe. For all I knew, Sebastian could have sent his mini army of hunters out in force. Keeping up appearances for the good of the academy seemed to be his top priority.

A scratching noise on the other side of the locked door tugged at my attention and I bristled. Ever since I'd had that conversation with Sebastian about him wanting to fix me, I'd been dreading his return. Every noise could mean the start of experimentation, injections or my ultimate demise.

However, it was Elizabeth who entered the room, dressed head to foot in black. She had pulled the hood of her jacket over her head to conceal her long blonde hair and had a staff strapped across her back. I couldn't help but grin up at her, relief flooding my chest. She looked like a cross between an avenging angel and a warrior.

'You are the best surprise I could ask for,' I said, jumping to my feet and pushing the uneaten dinner to one side.

'We thought you might want to get out of here,' she said, her voice shaking almost as much as her hands.

'We?'

Another figure entered the room, also dressed in black. Half expecting to see Adam's handsome face beneath the hood, I was shocked to spot Terry's mischievous grin.

'Terry? What the hell are you doing back here? Are you crazy?'

He chuckled and the sound came from deep in his throat. 'I volunteered to help Lizzie.'

I raised an eyebrow. 'Lizzie!'

'Oh yeah, we're BFFs now, aren't we, Liz?'

Elizabeth giggled as she pulled jeans and a jumper from a bag, dropping them on the bed with a pair of trainers and a torch.

'He has been incredibly helpful to our cause,' she said with a smile. 'Adam is on lookout upstairs and Miss Ross is in Dr Roberts's office keeping him busy, but I need you to get changed—and fast!'

Still reeling from the fact that Miss Ross was in on my daring rescue attempt, I stripped out of the hideous blue jumpsuit and wriggled into the clothes that Elizabeth had fetched. It felt good to be wearing my own clothes again.

I followed my friends out through the door. I was right; the room was in the basement and part of the maze of rooms that Elizabeth and I had explored the night we found Terry. The hospital wing was further in than we had ventured and consisted of a main office for Dr Wrinkly, a store room, and four patient rooms. All the hospital areas fed off a large circular space with direct access to the school through the main office. To any unsuspecting visitor, it was a fairly mundane hospital wing, but the seventh door, set into a dark alcove, led to the secret laboratory and all the horrors it held.

As we hurried through each section, I grew more and more anxious. If Sebastian found us, it could be bad for all of us. It wasn't only me who would end up in trouble—or dead. Sebastian would no doubt torture Terry, and Lizzie and Adam would be thrown out or maybe kept prisoner so they couldn't tell anyone about what was going on beneath the school.

We pushed through another door and entered the sterile room where we had discovered Terry chained to the gurney on our last visit. The silver tray, prepped with utensils, stood alongside a clean trolley with fresh folded linen on the end.

'Looks like they were all ready to start another experiment,' Terry said, holding the door open for us to walk through.

'It's for me,' I mumbled.

Elizabeth sucked in a breath and grabbed onto my hand.

'Sebastian wants to find out if I have werewolf DNA, and if I do, he is going to use a modified serum similar to the one he gave my mother.'

'We won't let him do that to you.' Elizabeth squeezed my hand. 'We'll get you out of here, I promise.'

Terry urged us forward and we navigated the rest of the maze with ease. Adam was waiting by the stock room door when we emerged into the academy foyer.

He held his finger up to his lips and motioned towards Sebastian's office door. The light shone through the glass, and I could hear muted voices coming from the room. Miss Ross's voice sounded louder than normal, and I realised she was either shouting at Sebastian or covering up our footsteps.

Elizabeth and Adam travelled the floor space across the foyer with ease, treading lightly to avoid any squeaky floorboards.

They beckoned me over and I looked to Terry for support.

'It's okay, I'm right behind you.'

I'd made it two steps when the office door flew open and Sebastian stormed through the opening. He hurtled towards me, his eyes blazing with rage.

'Do you think I'm that stupid to believe you wouldn't try and escape?' He grabbed my arm and I winced as his fingers tightened their grip.

Terry moved forward to intervene but Sebastian whirled me around, using me as a shield.

I saw Adam step out of the shadows, but I shook my head vehemently at him. I needed them to stay safe. He retreated back into the darkness.

With his free hand, Sebastian punched Terry hard in the face, causing him to stumble backwards and land heavily in the open doorway.

'Inside, both of you.' He shoved me through the door after Terry and then turned slowly on a stunned Miss Ross.

'You are dismissed, Miss Ross. I will deal with your indiscretions later, in accordance with the oath.' Sebastian's jaw was rigid as he spoke through gritted teeth. 'I think you've done quite enough for your goddaughter for one evening.'

I sucked in a sharp breath. It explained her need to help me discover the truth about my mum and her plans to protect me.

'Why didn't you tell me?' I whispered.

'I…I don't know,' she began.

Sebastian steered her to the exit, pushing her into the foyer, slamming the door and turning the key in the lock.

'No! Why did you do that?'

Sebastian turned his cold stare upon me and I stopped talking. Gone was the emotional man who had sobbed at my bedside. The man who stood in front of us was nothing but a monster.

He inclined his head at Terry but spoke to me. 'Am I to assume that you were the one who freed this creature from the lab?'

I stiffened and clenched my fists.

'He's *not* a creature, he's my friend.'

Sebastian laughed, the sound void of any humour.

'You don't honestly believe that, do you? Surely even you, Mia, can see how dangerous these beasts are. You've witnessed it firsthand.'

The images of Zak tearing Frank to pieces flashed through my mind.

'The pack protect their own,' I said, straightening my shoulders.

Sebastian was across the room before I could blink, his nose mere inches from mine.

'You are no wolf, Mia. Your genes follow the hunter line, *my* line, and you will do as I say because I. Am. Your. Father.'

Terry lunged forward, knocking Sebastian back a few steps.

'She's one of us and belongs with the pack. There's nothing you can do to stop me taking her.'

'Oh, really.' The glint in Sebastian's eye filled me with dread. Self-preservation kicked in and I took a step backwards, still reeling from the venom in his verbal attack.

He circled the desk and grabbed the phone from its cradle.

'It's me. Prepare the lab. I have two test subjects.'

I sat with my back to the wall, gripping my hands together so Terry couldn't see them trembling. Sebastian had stormed out after making his call, locking us inside his office. We tried to open the windows but they were sealed shut. It was hopeless.

'What are we going to do?' It was a stupid question because we were trapped. There was nothing we could do, but the silence freaked me out and I needed the comfort of conversation.

Terry slid down the wall to sit beside me.

'Don't worry, Mia. I'm sure Adam and Lizzie have found Zak by now and they're all on their way to rescue us.'

'Zak can't come here,' I gasped. 'It's too dangerous. If Sebastian gets hold of him, he'll end up with three test subjects.'

'Your brother will be careful. He's managed to keep an eye on you all these years without being discovered, hasn't he?'

I shrugged my shoulders. 'Why did he have to hide from me? My life was full of pain and anger and I could have done with a friend.'

'When Zak turned up at Joel's house, he was in bad shape. He didn't understand fully what was happening to him, why he was drawn to that town, that pack, and those people. Joel took him in, just like he did with the rest of us, and taught him the ways of the pack.'

Long shadows trailed across the office floor as I listened to Terry speak.

'He was a fast learner,' he said. 'Eventually he became Joel's second-in-command. He talked about you all the time and how he needed to keep you safe, but our pack was in constant threat from the hunters.'

'You mean, Hood Academy students?'

'Yes. It took all our efforts to keep ourselves safe. Zak sent me to check up on you from time to time. When I saw how you were being treated, I knew we had to do something.'

'How did you know?'

'I'd watch you on your way to school and you'd have a fresh bruise, or I'd hear the shouting from outside your house. Zak knew it was time to end it.'

'So he decided to kill Frank.'

Terry nodded.

'Why didn't he take me with him?'

'You're sixteen, Mia. You've come of age.'

The realisation dawned on me. 'I haven't turned.'

'No, you haven't. Zak thought you hadn't inherited the werewolf gene from your mum so he asked someone he could trust to help you instead.'

'Who?'

'Miss Ross. I only found out about her after you set me free from the lab. I had no idea Zak even had a contact at this place.'

So she *was* on our side. She had instigated everything because of her close friendship with my mum, and because Zak trusted her.

I smiled up at Terry. 'As messed up as all of this is, it's nice to think I had people fighting for me, even if I didn't know it at the time.'

He wrapped his muscular arm around my shoulder and hugged me tightly.

'I won't leave you, Mia. We'll protect each other, okay?'

'Okay.'

The door handle rattled as we heard the key turn in the lock. My stomach lurched. Was this the end? Was I about to die?

EIGHTEEN

ebastian stood in the doorway, silhouetted against the dim light cast from the lamps in the foyer. We scrambled to our feet, Terry pushing me behind him protectively.

'You don't have to do this,' he said, his voice nothing more than a whisper. 'She hasn't turned yet. There's every chance you're right and Mia is a hunter.'

'I can't afford to take that chance any more. I've dedicated my life to this school, to this project. I lost the woman I love. I've only just discovered that Mia is my daughter and I'm not prepared to let wolves take her from me too when we've got a lifetime to catch up on.'

I stepped around Terry so I was facing Sebastian, his colourless face and sunken cheeks guiding me to believe that he wasn't psychotic but only exhausted.

'I can help you, Mia,' he said.

'Like you helped my mum?'

'She understood what I was doing.'

'But did either of you ask if you should be doing it?' I said. 'The wolves only turn on a full moon and it's a night they spend enjoying nature, not killing. I have to work out where I belong, Sebastian, without your help. I don't know if I'm a werewolf or if I'm a hunter, but surely it's my choice to discover what I am in my own time.'

Sebastian shook his head. 'No, I can't risk you turning. I can't risk them finding out I have a werewolf daughter.'

'Who?'

'They'll ruin me. Take everything. Mr Parker will...'

'Wait!' The pieces started to come together. 'You're not bothered about me at all, are you? You're more worried about Felicity's father taking his funding from you.'

'I need that money!' he screamed. 'For you. To save *you*. It's what your mother wanted.'

I backed away, bumping into Terry who placed his big hand on my shoulder. I'd escaped one hellhole only to discover that I'd ended up in a worse situation. Sebastian was mad. Stark raving mad. I was going to die by his hand and yet he believed he was doing what was right for me.

I looked around frantically. We needed to get out of here and fast. Terry sensed my panic and grabbed my hand, squeezing my fingers to show me he was there supporting me.

'It's time to go,' Sebastian said right before a loud crack filled the air. He pitched to his knees, crumpling in a heap at our feet.

Out of the shadow of the doorway, Adam stepped forward swinging a cricket bat in his hand.

'Adam!' I launched myself at my friend, wrapping my arms around his neck. 'I'm so happy to see you.'

He chuckled. 'You didn't think I'd leave you in here, did you?'

Terry stepped over Sebastian's unconscious body and pulled me after him. As one we disappeared into the shadows and rushed to Adam's room to meet Elizabeth and Miss Ross.

'What now?' I asked.

SHELLEY WILSON

It was clear that I couldn't stay at Hood Academy, but suddenly I didn't want to leave. I looked around at the faces in front of me. Elizabeth's big blue eyes shone as they filled with tears. Adam's warm smile melted the fear that threatened to suffocate me, and Terry, the lone wolf who risked his life to save mine, waited patiently for me by the open patio doors leading to the gardens and the woods beyond.

I could smell the earth and the trees, and I longed to run across the lawn and disappear into the forest, but half my heart belonged here.

Elizabeth stepped forward and circled her arms around me. I squeezed her tightly and breathed in her scent, never wanting to forget the first friend I'd ever had.

'I'm going to miss you so much, Lizzie.'

'I know, but we'll stay in touch.'

She released her grip on me and wiped her eyes with the sleeve of her jacket. Adam put a supportive arm around her shoulders and I smiled up at him. I knew Elizabeth would be well taken care of.

Not wanting to leave without letting Adam know that he was as much a friend to me as Elizabeth, I flew at him and hugged him until he couldn't breathe.

'Look after her,' I whispered.

Miss Ross held her arms out wide and I allowed myself to be swallowed up in her embrace.

'If I am a werewolf, like my mum, then I'll accept that life and honour my pack because that's the right thing to do. It means we might never see each other again.'

I could feel my eyes filling up with tears, but I blinked them away.

'And if it turns out you're a hunter?'

I sighed deeply. 'If that's the case, I'll return, I promise. You can train me to be the best hunter you ever had, but I won't kill any wolves, or people, for you.'

OATH BREAKER

'I doubt Sebastian will allow you to return, Mia. He's a broken man. I'm not sure what the future holds for Hood Academy.'

'Maybe you can train me in secret.'

She laughed and held my face in her hands.

'It would be my honour.'

Terry coughed and pulled my attention to the open patio doors and the wilderness beyond.

'Time to go,' he said. 'We've got a long walk.'

I turned once more to Elizabeth and smiled. Tears poured down her beautiful face as she nodded at me. Adam stood close behind her as solid as ever.

'Take care of yourselves.'

•• • ● • ••

WE SHUFFLED OUT into the night air and I took a deep breath. The scents of the flowers flooded my senses and I relished the clear air after the oppressive academy.

With one last look at my friends, I joined Terry and began jogging across the lawn.

'It's a couple of hours' walk to the farmhouse,' Terry said. 'I'll race you if you like. Winner gets to have the first hot bath.'

I snickered and thumped his arm just as a loud crack filled the air. Terry stumbled next to me, falling to his knees and releasing an anguished cry. I had no time to comprehend what had happened before I heard Sebastian's voice calling my name.

I whirled around to see him rushing across the lawn with a gun in his hand. My head spun and I looked down at Terry who lay crumpled at my feet. Blood pooled on the lawn leaving a dark brown stain.

I grabbed at Terry's arm and helped him to his feet, his shoulder hanging forward as he tried to protect the wound. The bullet had travelled clean through his shoulder and blood coated his back and chest.

'I'm okay,' he said, his voice nothing more than a faint whimper. 'I'll heal, don't worry.'

I couldn't help but worry as I struggled to support his muscular frame. Another gunshot rang through the night air, and I felt the bullet brush past our heads as we limped towards the cover of the trees.

Sebastian shouted again. I looked behind me and saw Felicity and Elena sprinting across the lawn alongside him.

I unhooked myself from Terry and looked into his kind eyes.

'Go on without me. Get home so that your family can help you. I'll be right behind you, I promise.'

Terry faltered until I motioned towards the forest, urging him to escape before Sebastian could finish the job.

He gave a curt nod of his head then vanished into the trees.

I spun around to face the academy building and waited for Sebastian, Felicity and Elena to come to a halt a few feet away.

In the distance, I could see my friends moving out across the darkened grass, heading in my direction.

'I won't allow you to leave, Mia.' Sebastian's hand shook from the adrenalin of firing a gun. Sweat covered his face, and his hair was unkempt and matted with blood from the wound caused by the cricket bat.

'So you're going to shoot me?'

'It's what you deserve, wolf girl,' Felicity sneered at me, but I ignored her, keeping a wary eye on Sebastian and the gun in his hand.

'Just let me go,' I said. 'It's over, Sebastian.'

Under the pale light of the moon, he looked like a homicidal maniac. His eyes darted back and forth as he wrestled with his emotions.

Elena cried out as Elizabeth snuck up behind her, swiping her legs from under her and knocking her to the ground.

Felicity's head shot around at the sound and she leapt at Elizabeth, grabbing her arms and shaking my friend with such force I heard her teeth rattle. Adam didn't waste any time rushing to Elizabeth's aid, and in one fluid movement he elbowed

189

the redhead hard in the face. With my friends safe and rallying to support me, I turned my attention to the man who stood in front of me.

'I'm sorry,' he said.

Fear curled in my gut as he raised his gun, but before he could bring it up high enough to shoot, Miss Ross stepped out of the darkness and pressed the barrel of a shotgun to his temple.

Sebastian didn't say anything but the exhaustion that swept across his face confirmed his surrender. Adam rushed to take the gun from Sebastian's hand, smiling across at me as he rounded up Felicity and Elena.

'I've got this,' said Miss Ross. 'You're safe to leave now.'

I backed up towards the trees, watching the lights flicker on in the academy as the students and staff came to investigate the sounds of the gunshots.

I grinned at Elizabeth and Adam and lifted my hand in a silent salute. I let my gaze drift to Miss Ross, who was still holding the gun to Sebastian's temple. She gave me a wide smile. She had been friends with my mum and understood my need to discover who I was. It was her guidance that had led me to this place and I would remember her forever.

I was following my instincts just like my mum had done ten years ago and there was love and pride in Miss Ross's smile that filled me with hope.

Finally, I looked into Sebastian's dark eyes, and for the first time I saw my father looking back. Neither Sebastian nor Frank deserved my love or respect. They had both failed me, but it meant that I'd learned how to be strong.

I spun around and vanished into the forest without a backwards glance. I could hear Miss Ross snapping instructions at the approaching staff members, and the quiet sobs of my best friend. Felicity's shrill tone cut through the night air, and for a moment I worried that the redhead would rush after me, but Miss Ross's authoritative manner punctured her complaint and silenced her in an instant.

My eyes had adjusted to the darkness of the woods as I faced forward and pushed my way through the brambles and overhanging tree limbs. Before we left the safety of Adam's room, Terry had given me a brief outline of the route we were to take, just in case we were separated. It turned out to be a good idea. I had a long walk ahead of me, but there was a lightness in my heart that I'd never experienced.

I was free.

•• • ● • ••

STROLLING THROUGH THE woods after midnight had never been on my to-do list in my other life, but as I listened to the hoot of an owl and the rustling of nocturnal animals in the undergrowth, I began to feel more at peace. The further I walked, the more I was able to release the tension and anxiety that I'd felt at Hood Academy. Maybe I would end up returning one day, or maybe I would get to live out my days in the forest, surrounded by the beauty of nature and a new family.

After I'd been walking for over an hour I reached a winding lane. To my left rose a quaint farmhouse with walls of red brick and a roof of dark grey slate. A low white fence wrapped around the boundary, stretching towards a garage block. In the driveway I could see a truck with the Mills Family Farm sign emblazoned down the side.

Through the small cottage window, silhouetted against the lamplight, I could see Terry's outline. Byron was binding his shoulder with a strip of bandage as Cody looked on from over his shoulder. They were laughing and joking with one another and the sound travelled over to me, circling itself around my body and inviting me in.

A tall, muscular figure with longish brown hair that curled at the nape of his neck leant against the garden gate leading up to the house. His eyes twinkled in the moonlight as I approached, and a broad grin spread slowly across his face.

'Hey, Mia.'

I sprinted the rest of the way and flung myself at Zak. He wrapped his strong arms around me and spun me in a wide circle.

'Welcome home, little sister.'

ACKNOWLEDGMENTS

Thank you first and foremost to my parents for their unwavering support of everything I produce. Mum, you are the best saleswoman in the world. Thank you.

Thank you to my daughter's friend, Elizabeth, for the loan of your beautiful name—I hope our Elizabeth did you proud.

A huge thank you to the team at BHC Press for working on my book and turning it into a living entity. I'm pretty sure I shall continue to squeal with delight at every cover you produce for many years to come.

Thanks to my wonderful editor, Sooz, for believing in my story, guiding me when I had my dark moments, and patiently waiting for me to emerge from the treeline.

ABOUT THE AUTHOR

Shelley Wilson's love of fantasy began at the tender age of eight when she followed Enid Blyton up a *Magical Faraway Tree*.

Inspired by Blyton's make believe world, Shelley began to create her stories, weaving tales around faeries, witches and dragons.

Writing has always been Shelley's first love, but she has also enjoyed a variety of job roles along the way; from waitressing to sales and marketing and even working as a turkey plucker.

Shelley lives in the West Midlands, UK with her three teenage children, two fish and a dragon called Roger. She is at her happiest with a slice of pizza in one hand, a latte in the other and *Game of Thrones* on the TV. She would love to live in the Shire but fears her five foot ten inch height may cause problems. She is an obsessive list writer, huge social media addict and a full-time day dreamer.

www.shelleywilsonauthor.co.uk
www.bhcpress.com